The Barbados Effect

A SisterStay Escape Novella

Joi Jackson

The Barbados Effect

<h1 style="text-align:center">Chapter One</h1>

January

January Edwards stared at the cardboard box on her kitchen counter, thinking she should go through it and pick out the stuff from her office that she wanted to keep.

She'd tossed her belongings, mostly useless corporate swag and a few personal items, in the box on autopilot as she tried to process that she no longer had a job.

The PeachTech logo on a coffee mug mocked her from inside the box. She'd grabbed it without thinking, muscle memory from three years of reaching for it during endless product roadmap meetings.

"Due to organizational restructuring..."

The HR director's words from this afternoon still echoed in her head, delivered with the kind of practiced sympathy that came from firing a dozen people before lunch.

She should have thrown the mug at the man's head.

Apparently, three years of successful product launches, countless late nights debugging user flows with her work partner-in-crime, Cam, and a track record that spoke for itself meant nothing when the board decided to "pivot their strategy."

She snorted softly. Good luck with that.

A quarter of the company had gotten walking papers, and January knew that the remaining staff would have their hands full trying to do the work of everyone they'd just let go. But that wasn't her problem anymore.

She closed the box back up, deciding she'd deal with it later when she heard her phone buzz.

January pulled her phone from her purse and saw seven missed calls from her mother. Seven.

"Nope," she muttered, swiping the notification away. Brenda Edwards had an uncanny sense about family crises but her mother's particular brand of concern, which would inevitably morph into suggestions about how January should have seen this coming or what she should do next, was not what she needed after losing her job.

Another item on her to-do list that she wasn't dealing with right then: talking to her mother.

January tossed her phone back into her purse, as if burying it would somehow make her mother's calls disappear.

Now what? She glanced around at the walls of her townhouse. What did one do at two in the afternoon on a random Wednesday when they no longer had a job?

The responsible thing would be to update her resume. January walked to her home office and opened her laptop, pulling up the document she hadn't touched in three years.

The cursor blinked at the top of the page, like it was judging her. January squinted at her resume. The first bullet point said, "Strategic innovator..." She made a face. She barely remembered what that even meant. Her hand hovered over the keyboard, but her brain flatlined.

After a beat, January closed the laptop a little harder than necessary.

She wasn't doing this right now. Absolutely not.

The idea of job hunting, which she knew would be a full-time endeavor, felt like a weight on her chest.

Picking up her separation packet from the box, January thumbed through the pages as she walked to her living room and sank into her couch. The severance package was better than she expected: three month's salary. But was it enough time to find another product management position? With the holidays upon them, no one would be hiring for the next month. January let her head fall back against the couch, then grabbed the remote and flicked on the TV, needing noise to drown out the voice in her head predicting all the ways this could spiral into disaster. Her savings account could cover her mortgage and expenses for maybe three to four months if she was careful. Five if she ate nothing but ramen.

She winced. She hated ramen noodles.

A travel show filled the screen with some host with an annoyingly cheerful British accent standing on a pristine beach, turquoise water stretching behind her.

"...and that's why Barbados has become one of the ultimate destinations for solo female travelers seeking both adventure and sanctuary," the host was saying. "The island's year-round warmth isn't just about the weather, it's about the people, the culture, the feeling that you can truly be yourself here."

January almost changed the channel, but something in the woman's tone made her lower the remote. The host was interviewing someone now, a Black woman about January's age with sun-kissed goddess locs and an aura about her that was giving peacefulness and bliss.

"I came to Barbados after my divorce," the woman was saying. "I'd spent twenty years defining myself through my marriage, my job, other people's expectations. I needed to reclaim who I was."

January sat up straighter. The woman's words hit too close to home.

"And how did you make that journey safely as a solo traveler?" the host asked.

"I used an app called SisterStay. It connects women travelers with female hosts who offer more than just accommodation—they offer community. My host, Cheryl, didn't just give me a place to stay. She gave me a family of women who understood what it meant to rebuild yourself."

Rebuild yourself. The words echoed in January's mind.

When was the last time she'd done anything just for herself? Not for career advancement, not to meet someone else's expectations, but purely because she wanted to?

Leaning forward, January stabbed at the volume button on her remote.

"SisterStay has completely revolutionized how women travel alone," the host continued. "Each property is vetted, each host is a woman who's made her own brave journey, and every guest becomes part of a sisterhood that extends far beyond their stay."

The camera panned across a charming property with vibrant turquoise walls and white shutters, where women of different ages and ethnicities laughed together on a terrace overlooking ocean waves.

Something in January's chest tightened. She couldn't remember the last time she'd seen women look so free. So genuinely relaxed.

Before she could talk herself out of it, January grabbed her laptop and typed "SisterStay" into the browser. The website was beautiful and simple, with testimonials from women who'd found exactly what they needed:

"I arrived broken. I left whole."

"This wasn't just a vacation. It was a reset button on my life."

"For the first time in years, I remembered who I was before the world told me who I should be."

She clicked on "Barbados" almost without thinking. There were several properties, but one immediately caught her eye—a gorgeous small villa run by someone named Cheryl Evans, described as "a London expat who traded corporate life for Caribbean sunshine and never looked back."

January clicked on Cheryl's profile. The photo showed a woman with braids pulled into an elegant bun and a serene smile, standing on a sun-drenched veranda. Her bio read: "Former corporate lawyer on the partner track who burned out at forty. Started over at forty-two. Best decision I ever made."

Started over at forty-two.

January would be forty in less than three weeks. If this woman could start over at forty-two, surely January could figure something out at forty.

The villa had ten guest rooms, each with a private bathroom and a small balcony facing either the gardens or the sea.

A hammock strung between two tall palm trees sealed the deal. She could see herself sinking into that hammock watching the sunset while the ocean waves lulled her to sleep.

January clicked on the pricing and felt her stomach drop. It wasn't astronomical, but it wasn't cheap either. Two weeks at the property would take a chunk of her savings. That was money she should be conserving for mortgage payments and groceries while job hunting.

This was exactly the kind of impractical, irresponsible decision her mother would tell her not to make.

January clicked to close the tab with the website.

She should be practical. Update her resume. Start networking. Reach out to recruiters. Make a plan.

She re-opened the tab, thinking she'd check the dates. If the villa was booked, there was her answer.

The dates were available. Her severance package could cover it. She was turning forty in less than a month on January third. She could ring in the new year and her new decade doing something totally off brand for her: traveling alone to a new country just because.

Excitement coursed through her, and she jumped up to grab her credit card from her purse.

As she pulled her wallet out, January heard her phone buzz with a text. She pulled it out.

> CAM: Your mom called me. Put foot in mouth and she knows you lost your job 🙁

> You OK?

January stared at Cam's text, her thumb hovering over the keyboard. Of course her mother had called Cam. Brenda Edwards had a network of informants that would make the CIA jealous, and Cam had always been too polite to dodge her calls.

She typed and deleted three different responses then decided to keep it simple.

> JANUARY: I'm fine. Just need some space to figure things out.

His reply came immediately.

> CAM: She's worried…maybe let her know you're not injured or dead in a ditch somewhere. Also what about your birthday?

Right. The birthday. Brenda had been dropping hints about "special plans" for weeks, and January had been too buried in product roadmaps to pay attention. The thought of facing her family's concern, their questions about what came next, their careful optimism that she'd "land on her feet"—it felt impossible.

January closed her eyes and sighed. Her mother's "special plans" were notorious for being well-intentioned but often misaligned with what January actually wanted. Last year it had been a blind date with the son of someone from her mother's church.

JANUARY: Birthday TBD. Tell her I'm fine.

She looked back at the SisterStay website, at Cheryl's warm smile in the host photo, at the promise of a place where she could just be January, not January the Product Manager or January the Disappointment or January Who Should Have Her Life Together By Now.

She paused with her wallet in hand. This was crazy and impulsive. Financially questionable. Everything she wasn't.

But then again, being responsible and practical had just gotten her fired two weeks before Christmas.

What was the point of always playing it safe if it didn't keep you safe at all?

Her fingers moved across the keyboard, entering her credit card info before her brain could intervene.

Booking request for Sea La Vie, Barbados. Arrival: December 20th. Departure: January 4th.

January's finger hovered over the "Confirm Booking" button.

This was it. The point of no return.

She thought about all the extra hours she'd spent at work,

the box of belongings on her counter, the resume she couldn't bring herself to update. She thought about her milestone birthday looming and the expectations she'd spent thirty-nine years trying to meet.

She thought about the women in Barbados, peaceful and free.

January clicked "Confirm."

The confirmation email arrived within minutes, along with a personal note from Cheryl: "Welcome to the SisterStay family, January. I can't wait to meet you and share the magic of this special place. Safe travels, sister."

January stared at the screen, her heart pounding. She'd just booked a solo trip to a Caribbean island to stay in a strange house with people she didn't know. Three hours ago, she'd been a rational product manager with a five-year plan. Now she was apparently the kind of woman who made life-altering decisions based on travel shows and impulse.

Or maybe she was the kind of woman who finally gave herself permission to want something.

Her phone buzzed again.

> CAM: Whatever you need. I'm here.

She almost typed back that she was flying to Barbados in four days to figure out her life with the help of strangers. Almost. Instead, she put the phone down and started mentally cataloging what one packed for a two-week trip to reinvent herself.

January had no idea what came next.

But for the first time since walking out of that conference room, January felt something other than devastation.

She felt the tiniest spark of hope.

Chapter Two

Cam

Cameron Carter stared at his phone, reading January's text for the third time.

> JANUARY: I'm fine. Just need some space to figure things out.

He sighed, rubbing his jaw.

I'm fine.

Right. The woman who'd built her entire identity around being the best product manager at PeachTech was *fine* after getting unceremoniously dumped by the company she'd bled for. The same woman who'd stress-eaten an entire box of Girl Scout cookies from his desk during their last product launch was handling unemployment with perfect composure.

Cam knew January well enough to translate what *I'm fine* meant: *I'm falling apart but I'll die before I admit it.*

The layoffs had been quick and efficient, like a brutal corporate surgery. One minute they were all working on quarterly planning, the next minute HR was calling people into conference rooms. Cam had been in the break room when Ibrahim from January's product team walked past, box in hand, face blank with shock.

"They got the whole product team," Ibrahim had said quietly. "January, too."

Cam's stomach had dropped. He'd abandoned his coffee and headed straight for their floor, arriving just as January emerged from her cubicle with that damn cardboard box. She'd looked up, saw him, and something flickered across her face: hurt, embarrassment, determination, before the mask slammed back into place.

The guilt of that sat heavy in his chest now. Why had he survived the layoffs when someone as talented as January hadn't? She was better at her job than half the people they'd kept. The only difference was that her entire team had been "restructured" while his had been deemed "essential."

Corporate politics. That's all it was. And January had gotten caught in it.

He'd wanted to say something, but what did you say to your favorite co-worker when she'd just gotten gut-punched?

Sorry you got fired while I get to keep my job. Want to hang around till my day is over and grab a drink so we can talk about how unfair life is?

Instead, he'd stood there like an idiot, watching her walk out of his life with a cardboard box and her chin held high.

Now she wasn't answering her phone, and Brenda Edwards was about to call him for the second time today.

As if summoned by his thoughts, his phone rang. Brenda's smiling face filled the screen—a photo from last month when she'd insisted on taking a selfie after he'd helped her set up cloud storage for her photos.

"Hey, Miss Brenda," he answered, settling back in his desk

chair. The office was mostly empty now, but he hadn't been able to bring himself to leave. Going home to his quiet house meant accepting that January was really gone.

"Cameron, did you talk to January? She still hasn't called me back."

Cam closed his eyes.

He could hear the worry threading through her voice and he wanted to reassure her that January would be okay. Brenda had a way of adopting the people January cared about, and somehow Cam had become one of her honorary sons.

"She's... processing everything," Cam said carefully. "Today was really hard on her."

"Hard?" Brenda's voice rose an octave. "Cameron, what happened?"

Shit, shit, shit.

Had he really just outed January's firing to her mother? He'd assumed Brenda already knew. January told her mother everything—well, almost everything.

"I thought you knew," Cam said after a beat. "I thought January told you about the layoffs today at PeachTech." He swiveled his chair away from his computer screen, leaning forward with his elbows on his knees.

Silence stretched across the line, and Cam could practically hear Brenda's heart breaking through the phone.

"Layoffs?" Her voice came out shrill and on the brink of shrieking. "My baby lost her job?"

"Yeah," Cam said. "Her whole team was eliminated today."

"Well, no wonder I haven't heard from her today. She must be devastated. She should have called me."

"I'm sure there's a good reason she didn't tell you yet," Cam added quickly, trying to repair the damage. "It just happened a few hours ago."

"She's probably just in shock," Brenda said, her voice

softening. "January's always been so proud of her career. This must be hitting her hard."

"January's always been that way, ever since she was a little girl," Brenda continued. "She will never admit when something's wrong. Always tries to handle everything herself."

Cam nodded, forgetting Brenda couldn't see him. "That sounds like January."

"Oh, but this is perfect timing actually," Brenda said, her tone shifting from worry to determination. "She needs this party now more than ever."

Cam bit his lip. He was pretty sure the last thing January wanted was a birthday party when she had no job.

"Miss Brenda, I'm not sure—" he started.

"Cameron, I know what you're thinking, but hear me out. January needs to be reminded that her worth isn't tied to some corporate job. She needs to see how many people love her."

Cam rubbed the back of his neck. "I understand that, but maybe now isn't the best time for a surprise—"

"The party is in two weeks," Brenda continued. "I've already put deposits down on the caterer, the venue, everything. Her cousins are flying in from California. My sister and her husband are driving down from Tennessee."

Brenda had been planning this for months, calling him weekly with updates, asking his opinion on everything from the guest list to the menu. She'd been so excited, and so sure that surprising January with all the people who loved her would be the perfect way to start her new decade.

And Cam had gone along with it because he'd never been able to say no to Brenda Edwards. Because he'd thought a family celebration might be different from the office parties January avoided. Because he'd secretly hoped that maybe, in the glow of birthday happiness, he'd finally work up the courage to tell January how he felt.

He'd been a coward and an idiot.

"Maybe we should postpone—" Cam started.

"Absolutely not," Brenda said firmly. "That girl needs to know how loved she is, especially now. You mark my words, Cameron, if we let her hide away and feel sorry for herself, she'll spend her fortieth birthday alone in that townhouse eating ice cream and watching those awful shark movies."

The scary thing was, Brenda was probably right. January's default coping mechanism was isolation, and losing her job would only make that worse.

"I just don't think she's in the headspace for a party right now," Cam said.

"Which is exactly why it needs to be a surprise. If we ask her, she'll say no and spend the day wallowing. But if we surprise her with everyone who loves her, show her that her worth isn't tied to some corporate job..." Brenda's voice softened. "She needs this, sweetheart. She needs to remember who she is outside of work."

Cam rubbed his forehead, where a headache was building. The thing was, he agreed with Brenda. January did need to remember her worth and to be surrounded by love. But she also needed space to process her grief and ambushing her with a party felt like the opposite of what she'd asked for.

He thought about last month when someone from HR had sent a company-wide email announcing the birthdays in January—one of those cheerful messages about celebrating team members with cake in the break room at three o'clock. Cam had been at his desk when he'd heard her swear softly and gather her laptop. He'd found her ten minutes later in the stairwell, sitting on the steps with her laptop open, clearly hiding. "You okay?" he'd asked.

"I specifically asked HR not to do that," she'd said, her voice tight. "I don't need the whole company singing happy birthday to me while I eat grocery store sheet cake and pretend to be grateful."

"Most people like being celebrated," Cam had offered carefully.

"I'm not most people." She'd looked up at him, and he'd seen something raw in her expression. "I just...I don't like being the center of attention like that. I feel like I'm on display, like everyone's judging whether I'm reacting the right way."

She'd skipped the break room celebration entirely, claiming back-to-back meetings. Cam had saved her a piece of cake and left it on her desk with a sticky note: "For later. No audience required."

He should tell Brenda that. He should be January's advocate right now, protecting her boundaries even when she wasn't here to do it herself.

But Brenda was already talking about the menu, the DJ she'd hired, and how much January's aunt was looking forward to seeing her.

"Did she say anything about her plans?" Brenda asked. "For her birthday, I mean?"

"She said birthday plans were TBD," he said instead.

"See? She doesn't have any plans because she's given up. We can't let her spend her fortieth birthday alone, Cameron. Promise me you'll keep working on her. You're the only one she might actually listen to."

The faith in Brenda's voice made his chest tight. When his own parents had moved to Arizona two years ago, citing better weather and lower cost of living, Brenda had somehow stepped into the gap they'd left. She remembered his birthday, asked about his projects at work, invited him to family barbecues and holiday dinners. She'd become the closest thing to family he had in the city.

Now she was asking him to choose between honoring

January's clearly stated need for space and keeping a promise to the woman who'd made him feel less alone in the world.

"I'll...see what I can do," he said.

"That's my boy. Oh, and Cameron? I know you care about her. More than just as a friend."

Cam heaved a sigh. "Miss Brenda—"

"Honey, I've got eyes. The way you look at my daughter, the way you always make sure she eats lunch, how you light up when she walks into a room? That's not just colleague behavior."

Heat crept up Cam's neck. Was he really that obvious?

"She doesn't see it," he said quietly.

"January's brilliant about everything except what's right in front of her face," Brenda said with a gentle laugh. "But maybe her birthday could be the perfect time for both of you to stop hiding."

After they hung up, Cam sat in the darkening office, staring at the whiteboard with January's neatly written process diagram.

Tomorrow he'd have to come back to this office and pretend everything was normal, while January would be...what? Job hunting? Spiraling into self-doubt? The unfairness of it made his stomach churn.

He thought about the moment three years ago when they'd first been partnered on a product launch. January had been intimidating, whip-smart, driven, completely focused on excellence. But during their third late-night planning session, when she'd ordered pizza for the whole team and insisted everyone go home at a reasonable hour despite the deadline pressure, he'd seen the heart underneath all that professional armor.

He'd been falling for her ever since, one small kindness at a time.

The way she'd stayed late while he debugged a particularly stubborn piece of code. How she'd brought him soup and office gossip when he'd been sick, claiming she "happened to be nearby" even though she lived twenty minutes away. The soft smile she got when she thought no one was looking, usually while reading emails from her family.

He remembered the exact moment he'd known for sure. Eight months ago at a company offsite in Nashville. They'd been stuck in the hotel bar after a particularly tedious strategy session and January had been on her third glass of wine, more relaxed than he'd ever seen her.

"Cam, you know what I miss?" she'd said, swirling the wine in her glass. "I miss having time to just exist. Not be productive, not be strategic, just be."

"I feel you. When was the last time you did that?" he'd asked.

She'd thought about it for a long moment. "I genuinely don't remember."

The sadness in her voice had broken something in him. He'd almost said it right then—that he was falling in love with her, that he'd take her anywhere she wanted to go just to see her truly happy, that she deserved so much more than what she was giving herself.

But then her phone had buzzed with a work email, and the moment had passed. And Cam had convinced himself it was for the best. They worked together. She had rules. He'd respected that.

Now those rules didn't apply anymore, and Cam had no idea what to do with that information.

Two weeks ago when she'd laughed at one of his terrible coding jokes and he'd realized he wanted to spend the rest of his life making her laugh like that.

But January Edwards didn't date coworkers. She'd made

that crystal clear during their first team happy hour when Vincent from Sales had tried to ask her out.

"Professional boundaries are very important to me," she'd said, politely but firmly declining Vincent's invitation to dinner. "I don't blur those lines."

The message had been clear enough that Cam had never even tried. He'd convinced himself that their friendship was more valuable than risking rejection.

But January wasn't his coworker anymore.

Cam stared at his phone, hoping for another text, some sign that she was okay. But the screen remained dark. Whatever January was planning, he feared she was going to attempt to do it alone.

He started typing a message, then deleted it. What could he possibly say that would help? That would bridge the gap between his survivor's guilt and her devastation?

Finally, he typed:

Whatever you need. I'm here.

But as he hit send, Cam realized that being "here" might not be enough. January was pulling away from everyone who cared about her, building those walls higher with every hour that passed.

Chapter Three

January

The Grantley Adams International Airport in Barbados was nothing like the sterile, fluorescent-lit terminals January was used to. Even inside the building, she could feel the island's warmth seeping through the walls, and the melodic accents of the baggage handlers made her shoulders relax for the first time in days.

She'd barely slept on the early morning flight from Atlanta, her mind ping-ponging between excitement and terror about what she'd just done.

Five days ago, she'd been a product manager with a steady paycheck and a five-year plan. Now she was unemployed in a foreign country, running away from her problems like some kind of romance novel heroine having a breakdown.

Except this was her life, not a novel, and she still had no idea what she was doing.

Her phone buzzed as she wheeled her suitcase toward the taxi stand.

> MOM: Safe travels, baby. Call me when you
> get to where you're staying so I know you
> made it okay.

January smiled despite her nerves. She'd finally called her mother back on Thursday, after a night of avoiding the inevitable conversation. Her mother had been hurt that January hadn't called immediately after losing her job but said she understood once January explained she'd needed time to process the shock.

The conversation had been harder than January expected. Her mother's disappointment, not in January, but for her, had been palpable through the phone.

"You gave that company everything," Brenda had snapped. "And this is how they repay you?"

"Mom, it's just business. Restructuring happens."

"Don't you dare defend them, January Edwards. You're allowed to be angry."

But January wasn't sure she was still angry. Mostly she felt numb. Like someone had scooped out the part of her that knew who she was and what she was supposed to be doing.

When she'd told her mother about her impulsive decision to fly to Barbados, she'd braced for a lecture about responsibility and finances. Instead, her mother simply sighed and said, "Maybe this is exactly what you need right now, January. You've been working yourself to death for years. Take a few days to rest and recharge."

January hadn't corrected her mother's assumption about the length of the trip. She'd let Brenda believe it was just a long weekend getaway, not a two-week escape that would take her through Christmas and her fortieth birthday. The guilt of that omission sat heavy in her chest, but she'd known that if she told the whole truth, Brenda would have talked her out of it.

Her mother had been surprisingly supportive, even excited about the trip. "Barbados sounds nice! Maybe I'll drag your father there for our anniversary. But you deserve some sunshine after the week you've had."

Now, stepping into the warm Barbados air, January pushed down the guilt about misleading her mother about her plans. She'd deal with family expectations later. Right now, she just needed to breathe.

The taxi driver was a chatty man named Winston who pointed out landmarks as they drove through the island. "First time to Barbados?"

"Yes. I'm staying at a place called Sea La Vie?"

Winston's face lit up. "Ah, you're going to Miss Cheryl's place! She's good people. Came here from London about five years ago, bought that old property and fixed it up real nice. You'll love it there."

Twenty minutes later, the taxi pulled up to a beautiful turquoise building with white shutters and a wraparound veranda. Bougainvillea climbed the walls in brilliant purple cascades, and the sound of waves was audible from the front garden. It looked exactly like the website photos, but somehow more magical in person.

A woman emerged from the front door before January had even paid the taxi driver. She was tall and elegant, with beautiful long braids adorned with small gold cuffs and rich brown skin that glowed with health. She looked to be in her early forties, with an easy confidence and a smile that was both warm and genuine.

"You must be January! I'm Cheryl. Welcome to Sea La Vie."

Cheryl's British accent was softened by years of island living, and there was something immediately calming about her presence. She helped January with her bags and led her up the front steps.

"I have to say, when I got your booking, I was so pleased. We love hosting women who are brave enough to travel solo and discover what they're made of."

Brave. January almost laughed. She didn't feel brave. She felt like she was running away.

The interior of the house was as charming as the exterior. Colorful local artwork adorned the creamy white walls, and the furniture looked comfortable rather than precious. Everything felt designed for relaxation.

And for the first time in five days, January felt like she could actually exhale.

"I have you in the Indigo Room," Cheryl said, leading January up a polished wooden staircase. "It has a balcony and a beautiful view of the ocean. You'll be sharing the house with two other guests who recently arrived: Kelsi and Monica."

The Indigo Room was perfect: A queen bed with white linens, a small writing desk by the window, and French doors that opened onto a balcony overlooking the beach. January could see the hammock she'd admired on the website strung between two palm trees.

"This is beautiful," January said, meaning it.

"I'm so glad you like it. Now, I always tell my guests...this house runs on island time, which means you do whatever feels right for your soul. If you want to sleep until noon, sleep until noon. If you want to sit on the beach and cry, that's perfectly fine too. If you need to talk, I'm here. If you need solitude, we respect that."

January felt her eyes prick with unexpected tears. "Thank you."

When was the last time someone had given her permission to do whatever felt right for her soul?

"We do a happy hour every weekday evening from five to seven, feel free to join us. Monica and Kelsi are lovely, and I think you'll find kindred spirits here." Cheryl continued. "Though I have to admit, I've been thinking about expanding what we offer here. The hospitality industry in Barbados is so competitive, and I keep wondering if there are other ways to create memorable experiences for our guests."

January's business instincts immediately perked up. "What kind of expansion were you thinking about?"

Cheryl's eyes lit up with interest. "Well, for instance, our guests are always asking where they can buy authentic Bajan products to take home—local soaps, oils, things like that. I know amazing local artisans, but there's no good way to connect them with tourists. And honestly, I came from corporate law, not hospitality. I'm still learning the business side."

"That's actually a really interesting market gap," January found herself saying. "You have a captive audience of women travelers who are probably looking for authentic experiences and products. Have you thought about partnerships with local suppliers, or maybe developing your own product line?"

"I've thought about it, but I wouldn't know where to start. Product development, marketing, distribution—it's all foreign to me." Cheryl paused at the top of the stairs. "What's your background? You sound like you know business."

"I was a product manager at a tech company," January said, then quickly corrected herself. "Well, I was until this week."

Cheryl's expression softened with understanding. "Ah. That explains the solo travel to figure things out. Well, if you're ever interested in an informal conversation about business strategy, I'd love to pick your brain. But for now, let me let you get settled."

After Cheryl left, January stood on her balcony, breathing in the warm air that carried hints of salt and tropical flowers. For the first time in days, the knot in her chest began to loosen. But her mind was already spinning with possibilities—local sourcing, authentic product lines, guest experience enhancement. Maybe this crazy impulse trip wasn't such a terrible idea after all.

Her phone buzzed with a text.

> CAM: Coffee this morning?

January stared at the message, her thumb hovering over the keyboard. She and Cam often met up at a local coffee shop on Saturday mornings after her spin class. She should tell him where she was, share this moment of peace she'd found. But something held her back.

He would want to know all the details, why she had run off so suddenly. He'd probably try to fix things, convince her to come home, remind her about her mother's mysterious birthday plans.

Cam was tied to her old life, to the job she'd lost, to the expectations she was trying to escape.

> JANUARY: Sorry, can't today. Enjoy your weekend. We'll talk soon, I promise.

She'd call him later when she'd had some time to settle in. In the meantime, she would explore the house.

Downstairs, she found a young woman arranging fresh flowers in the main living area. She looked to be in her early twenties, with warm brown skin and her hair pulled back in a neat bun. She was humming a tune while carefully positioning birds of paradise and hibiscus in a tall vase, stepping back periodically to assess her work.

"Those are beautiful," January said.

The young woman looked up with a bright smile. "Thank you! I'm Jianna. I help Miss Cheryl run Sea La Vie. You must be January—I saw your name on the arrival list."

"Nice to meet you, Jianna. How long have you been working here?"

"About a year now. I'm studying hospitality management at the University of the West Indies, and Miss Cheryl lets me work here part-time to get real-world experience." Jianna's pride in her work was evident in her voice. "She's taught me so much about running a boutique property."

January felt a familiar spark of interest, the same feeling she got when mentoring junior team members at PeachTech. Or had gotten. That was all in her past now.

The reminder stung, but she pushed it aside.

"What's been your favorite class so far?"

"The marketing class." Jianna's enthusiasm was infectious. "We have done a lot of case studies of real-world companies but sometimes I feel like the examples in our textbooks don't really apply to a small property like this."

January found herself leaning forward, genuinely curious. "What are your career goals once you've gotten your degree?"

"I'd love to run my own property someday. Maybe not exactly like this one, but something that serves women who need a safe space to figure things out." Jianna's eyes lit up with enthusiasm. "Miss Cheryl says I have good instincts for hospitality, but I know I have so much more to learn about the business side—operations, marketing, guest experience management."

January felt the familiar itch to share knowledge, to help someone navigate their career path. It was the same instinct that had made her a natural mentor to junior product managers.

But was she even qualified to give career advice anymore? She'd just gotten fired.

The thought must have shown on her face because Jianna tilted her head with concern. "You okay?"

"Yeah, sorry." January forced a smile. "What kind of marketing have you studied so far?"

For the next hour, they talked about everything from social media strategy to guest retention programs. January grew more excited as she shared insights from her product management experience—how to understand your target market, how to create experiences that exceeded expectations, how to build systems that could scale.

It felt good. Natural. Like maybe she still had value even without the PeachTech job title.

"You know so much about business," Jianna said, clearly impressed. "What do you do for work?"

January hesitated. "I was a product manager at a tech company. 'Was' being the operative phrase." Saying the words hurt more than she wanted to admit.

"Oh, I'm sorry. Are you between jobs right now?"

"Something like that." January managed a smile. "Which is partly why I'm here. Trying to figure out what comes next."

And wasn't that the truth. She had no idea what came next. No plan, no strategy, no roadmap. Just this desperate need to be somewhere that wasn't home, where she didn't have to face the reality of her failure quite yet.

"Well, if you ever want to talk more about business strategy or marketing, I'd love to learn from someone with your experience," Jianna said. "Miss Cheryl is amazing with the hospitality side, but she admits she's still figuring out the business development piece."

"I'd be happy to," January said, surprised by how good it felt to be asked for her expertise. At PeachTech, she'd been just another employee. Here, her knowledge felt valuable in a different way.

"The other guests are down on the beach if you'd like to

meet them," Jianna said, glancing toward the ocean. "Kelsi and Monica. They're both really nice."

January glanced toward the beach, where she could see two figures walking along the shore, then back at Jianna's bright, expectant face.

"Maybe later," January said. "I'm going to settle in first."

Jianna nodded with understanding. "No pressure. They'll be around."

January watched the young woman return to her flowers, humming softly. For the first time in days, January felt like she could relax. She didn't know what came next, didn't have a plan or answers to the inevitable questions about her life.

But here, in this moment, helping someone find their path felt like more than enough.

Chapter Four

Cam

Monday morning felt different the moment Cam walked into the PeachTech office. The usual hum of activity was muted, desks that had been occupied just a week ago now sat empty with dark computer monitors and abandoned coffee mugs. The layoffs had left visible scars throughout the building.

But it was January's empty desk that made his chest ache.

Cam had gotten used to seeing her workstation before his own with her neat stacks of product specifications, the small succulent plant she somehow kept alive despite her tendency to forget everything except work deadlines, her coffee mug with the PeachTech logo. Now there was just vacant space where his work partner used to sit.

Her absence felt like a physical thing, a hole in the office that no amount of reorganization could fill.

He pulled out his phone and scrolled through his recent texts with January. The last exchange had been Saturday morning, when he'd asked if she wanted to grab coffee.

She'd given him a vague response.

Sorry, can't today. Enjoy your weekend. We'll talk soon, I promise.

What exactly did "soon" mean?

Three days? A week? A month? Cam sighed and tossed his phone onto his desk, the clatter drawing a few glances from the survivors of the corporate purge.

Now it was Monday morning, and her desk looked like a museum exhibit of her former life. Cam tried calling her cell phone, but it went straight to voicemail.

"January, it's Cam. Just wanted to check in and see how you're doing. Call me back when you get this."

By lunchtime, worry had morphed into genuine concern. January was methodical about everything, including staying in touch with people she cared about. For her to disappear completely without explanation meant something was seriously wrong.

Before he could spiral further, his phone rang. Brenda's name flashed on the screen. Maybe January had finally called her mother.

"Hey, Miss Brenda."

"Cameron, sweetheart, I need to talk to you." Her voice was tight with barely controlled panic. "Have you talked to January lately?"

Cam's relief evaporated. "No, I was hoping you had. She's not answering her phone."

"Cameron, January's in Barbados and said she's staying until after the first of the year."

"She's what?" Cam nearly dropped his phone. "Did you say Barbados?"

"Yes, she flew out Saturday. Said she needed to clear her head after losing her job." Brenda's voice was strained. "I thought it was just for a few days, but I just called her and... Cameron, she's not coming home for Christmas."

Cam felt his stomach drop. January had left the country without telling him. While he'd been worried about her not returning his texts, she'd been on a plane to the Caribbean.

"She's staying through New Year's. Through her birthday!" Brenda's voice cracked. "I don't understand what's gotten into her. This isn't like January. I thought this was just a long weekend trip to clear her head, but she's planning to spend Christmas on some island with strangers instead of her family."

Cam closed his eyes, pieces clicking into place. January wasn't just taking a few days to decompress—she was running away from everything, including the surprise birthday party Brenda had been planning for months.

"She's probably just processing everything that happened," he said carefully. "Losing her job was a big blow."

"That's exactly why she needs to be home with people who love her, not hiding on some beach!" Brenda's maternal frustration was palpable. "Cameron, I'm worried about her. She's never missed Christmas with the family, and her fortieth birthday... we've had these plans for months."

"What do you want me to do?" he asked, though he was starting to suspect where this conversation was heading.

"I want you to go get her."

"Miss Brenda—"

"Cameron, you're the only one she might listen to. She trusts you," Brenda said. "You've got convince her to come back home for the party."

Cam stared at his phone. "You want me to go to Barbados?" He stood up from his desk, running a hand over his hair. "I can't just—"

"You said you have time off. You can get her to come home," Brenda pressed.

Cam walked to the break room, needing privacy for this conversation. The space was empty, everyone else at lunch or hiding at their desks like he'd been.

"She needs space to figure things out," he said.

"She needs her family. She needs to be surrounded by people who love her."

Brenda's voice softened into the tone she used when she was about to ask for a favor. "I'll pay for your flight. And your hotel. Whatever it costs."

He sighed. This was a bad idea, wasn't it?

"Miss Brenda, I appreciate it, but—"

"No buts. I'm the one asking you to do this. Let me at least cover your flight."

Cam hesitated. He could accept that. The flight was one thing. But the hotel, that he'd handle himself.

"Okay. The flight. But I'll cover everything else."

"Cameron—"

"Please, Miss Brenda. Let me do this."

There was a pause, then Brenda sighed. "Okay. But you call me if you need anything else. Anything."

After they hung up, Cam stood in the empty break room, his mind racing. Barbados. She'd gone all the way to Barbados.

He pulled out his phone and opened Instagram, something he rarely did. Maybe she'd posted something that would give him a clue about where exactly she was, or how she was really doing.

Her profile loaded, and there it was: a photo posted three hours ago. A beach at sunset, turquoise water and palm trees silhouetted against an orange sky. The caption read: "Sometimes you have to get lost to find yourself."

The location tag said Barbados.

Cam stared at the photo. She looked peaceful. Or at least, the sunset looked peaceful. But that caption, "get lost to find yourself" sounded like someone running away, not someone finding anything.

Brenda was asking him to fly to a foreign country to convince January to come home for a surprise party she didn't know about. It was completely insane.

But the alternative was letting January spend Christmas and her fortieth birthday alone, convinced that nobody cared enough to come after her.

Was she finding herself? Or was she just running away?

And if he followed her, was he respecting her boundaries or violating them?

His manager, Jeff, poked his head into the break room. "Hey, Cam, there you are. Listen, if you don't have anything pressing going on, you can start your holiday vacation early. Company's closed Christmas Day through New Year's, but I can give you a few extra days if you want. Things are pretty dead around here anyway."

Cam looked up, January's sunset photo still glowing on his phone.

"Yeah, actually. I could use some time," Cam said absently. Maybe extra time off would let him figure out what was going on with January.

"Why don't you wrap up today and take the rest of the week off? We'll see you back on the fifth."

Cam checked his calendar. With the extra days and the company holiday, he was looking at nearly two weeks off.

"Thanks, Jeff." Cam rubbed his hands together. Two weeks. That was enough time to—

To what? Fly to Barbados and track down a woman who clearly didn't want to be found?

"I appreciate it."

"Enjoy the holidays, you've worked hard this year to improve the team's output," Jeff said before he left.

Cam nodded, but his mind was already elsewhere.

His phone buzzed with a text from his cousin Toya, who worked at a travel agency in Buckhead.

> TOYA: Cam! Heard about the layoffs at your company on the news. You good?

An idea began to form.

> CAM: Still got a job but I need a favor. Any way you can get me a deal on a last-minute trip to Barbados?

> TOYA: Barbados? Sir, that's going to be expensive this close to Christmas.

> CAM: I know. It's important.

> TOYA: Let me see what I can do. When do you need to leave?

Cam looked back at his calendar. If he left Wednesday morning, he'd have over a week.

> CAM: Wednesday if possible.

> TOYA: 😳😳😳

> TOYA: You're gonna owe me big time. Give me an hour.

An hour later, Toya called back. "Okay, if you get World Cup tickets from your company again, I'm your plus one."

Cam grimaced. An email had gone out about the upcoming World Cup semi-finals being hosted in Atlanta. The company was offering tickets, but employees had to work company-sponsored events in order to get them. Which meant he'd have to man their corporate booth at some point and act like he loved being there.

"Fine. Did you find me a good deal?"

"Flight's reasonable. I got you on a last-minute deal with Caribbean Airlines. But hotels are brutal right now. Everything decent is booked solid or charging Christmas rates."

"How brutal?" Cam asked, already dreading the answer.

"The only thing I could find that's not completely sketchy is Sandy Lane, and that's because they had a last-minute cancellation. But Cam..." Toya's voice took on the tone she used when delivering particularly bad news to clients. "It's Sandy Lane."

"Okay? Is that supposed to mean something to me?"

"Bruh, you really don't know anything about Barbados, do you?" Toya laughed. "Sandy Lane is like...imagine the fanciest resort you can think of, then multiply it by ten. We're talking about where celebrities go to hide from paparazzi. Tiger Woods got married there. It's the kind of place that has its own golf course and the staff remembers your name after one visit."

Cam's heart sank. "So we're talking about mortgage payment territory?"

"We're talking about your entire paycheck territory," Toya said. "Like, the kind of place where they don't even put prices on the menu."

"Why Sandy Lane though? Isn't there anything more... normal?"

"Trust me, I looked everywhere. Christmas week in Barbados? You're lucky to find a cardboard box on the beach." Toya's keyboard clicked in the background.

"This one is only available because of a cancellation. I got a homegirl that specializes in luxury Caribbean travel and she got us a lower rate...you want me to book it?"

Cam pulled up his banking app, staring at his savings

account. He'd been putting money aside for over a year for his dream trip to Japan. Cherry blossoms in Kyoto, ramen in Tokyo, hiking Mount Fuji. He'd even bought a phrase book and had been practicing basic Japanese on his lunch breaks.

One week at Sandy Lane would wipe out most of it.

But what was Japan compared to January?

"It's a garden room view in the Orchid area," Toya continued. "Rate is about half what it would normally be."

"Half the normal rate is still insane," Cam muttered, but he could hear himself weakening. The cherry blossoms would bloom next year. And the year after that.

January needed him now.

Cam thought about January, probably sitting on a beach somewhere, convincing herself that nobody cared enough to come after her. He thought about Brenda, desperate to show her daughter how loved she was. He thought about his own cowardice over the past three years, always finding reasons not to tell January how he felt.

Maybe it was time to stop finding reasons not to act.

"Book it."

"You sure? This is going to hurt your wallet."

"Book it, Toya. And I guess I owe you World Cup tickets now."

"Damn right you do. I'll send you the confirmation details. Flight leaves Wednesday morning at eight-thirty. And Cam, pack some nice clothes...Sandy Lane has a dress code."

After hanging up, Cam sat in the break room, staring at the confirmation email that had just arrived. Flight booked. Hotel booked. Two weeks off approved.

He was really doing this. Flying to Barbados to find January and convince her to come home for a party she didn't know about.

It was either the bravest thing he'd ever done or the stupidest.

His phone buzzed with a text from Brenda.

BRENDA: Did you decide? Can you go?

Cam looked at the confirmation email again, then at January's Instagram photo. The sunset. The palm trees. The promise of finding yourself.

CAM: I'm going. Flight leaves Wednesday. You're covering the flight. I've got the rest.

BRENDA: Oh thank God. Thank you, Cameron. You're an answer to prayer. Let me know how much to send you for the flight.

And Cameron, remember she's lucky to have you in her life.

CAM: I can't promise I'll convince her to come back.

BRENDA: Just make sure she knows she's loved. That's all I ask.

Cam closed his eyes. Make sure she knows she's loved. He could do that.

Even if he couldn't bring himself to tell her he was the one who loved her.

Chapter Five

January

January had never realized how much she loved Christmas markets until she found herself wandering through the one in Holetown on Christmas Eve morning.

The air was warm and sweet with the scent of sugar cakes baking in portable ovens and rum punch laced with nutmeg and cinnamon. Steel drum renditions of "Silent Night" and "Joy to the World" mixed with soca music drifted from speakers strung between towering royal palm trees, while vendors called out cheerful greetings in melodic Bajan accents.

"You should go! You have to try the conkies," Jianna had insisted over breakfast, her eyes lighting up as she described them. "They're like little parcels of heaven...cornmeal and coconut and sweet potato all mixed up with spices, then wrapped in banana leaves and steamed. Ms. Desiree makes the best ones on the island, and she only sells them at the Christmas market."

January had been hesitant to leave the peaceful cocoon of

Sea La Vie, but Cheryl had practically pushed her out the door. "A day out will do you a world of good, love. You can't experience Barbados from the villa alone."

Now, as she wandered past stalls selling handmade ornaments carved from local coral stone and vendors offering samples of black cake soaked in rum, January marveled at how different this felt from Christmas in Atlanta. Back home, December 23rd would have meant a frantic day of last-minute shopping at crowded malls, rushing from one grocery store to another to help her mother prepare for the family gathering. January would have been checking items off lists, wrapping presents with precision, and fielding her mother's stressed calls about whether they had enough chairs or if they'd gotten enough sweet potatoes. Christmas Eve in Atlanta meant obligation, scheduling, and the constant worry that something would go wrong.

Here, time moved differently. She watched an elderly man carefully arranging bottles of homemade pepper sauce in perfect rows, stopping frequently to chat with customers about the family recipes passed down through generations. A woman at the next stall who appeared to be in her seventies, swayed gently to the music as she arranged displays of Christmas pudding and sweet bread, calling out "Merry Christmas, darling!" to everyone who passed.

"You trying some sorrel, sweetheart?" asked a vendor with silver locs and a smile that crinkled her entire face. She offered January a small cup of the deep red drink. "Made it fresh this morning with ginger and cloves. Perfect for Christmas morning."

January accepted the cup, savoring the spicy-sweet flavor that seemed to embody the warmth of the island itself. "It's delicious. What's the tradition behind it?"

"Oh, we been making sorrel for Christmas since my

grandmother's time," the woman explained, ladling more into cups for other customers. "The hibiscus flowers, they only bloom this time of year. Christmas wouldn't be Christmas without sorrel and black cake."

January bought a bottle to take back to Sea La Vie, charmed by the woman's easy conversation and the way she seemed to have all the time in the world for every customer. No rushing, no stress about getting to the next task. Just the simple pleasure of sharing something special with strangers who were, for this moment, part of her extended Caribbean Christmas family.

As she continued through the market, January found herself relaxing in a way she hadn't in years.

The morning had been exactly what she needed. She'd bought conkies from Ms. Desiree (Jianna was right—they were heaven), sampled fresh fruit from a cheerful vendor who'd insisted she try starfruit, and found a beautiful handwoven basket for her mother as a peace offering.

She was examining a pair of turquoise earrings she knew her mother would love, handcrafted by a woman with intricate braids and the warmest smile January had ever seen, when movement caught her eye across the crowded market square.

A man in khaki pants and a white linen shirt was talking to one of the jewelry vendors, his head tilted in that focused way that suggested he was asking serious questions. The sleeves of his shirt were rolled up to his elbows, exposing strong forearms, and dark sunglasses covered his eyes. He was holding what appeared to be a to-go bag of food.

January continued to stare. The man was gorgeous: tall, dark, and lean with broad shoulders that filled out his shirt perfectly. Dark, close-cropped hair that looked like he'd just stepped from the barber chair, and even with the sunglasses hiding his eyes, she could see the intensity in his posture. The kind of man who looked like he knew exactly what he wanted and how to get it.

Heat crept up her neck as her gaze lingered on the way the linen fabric moved against his back when he leaned forward to listen to the vendor's response, how his rolled sleeves revealed the corded muscles of his forearms as he gestured. God, it had been way too long since she'd allowed herself to appreciate an attractive man. Work had consumed so much of her life that she'd forgotten what it felt like to have her pulse quicken just from looking at someone.

The man turned slightly, giving her a better view of his profile, and January's heart did a little dance. Strong jawline, concentration creasing his brow as he nodded at whatever the vendor was telling him. She found herself envisioning an island fling...no strings, no promises that could be broken.

Then he lifted his sunglasses to get a better look at something the vendor was showing him, and January's mouth dropped open.

Cam? Her Cameron from work was here? Her best friend and work partner who had somehow followed her to Barbados and was standing in a Christmas market looking like he'd stepped out of a steamy beach romance novel while she was having completely inappropriate thoughts about his forearms?

"Oh my God," she breathed, ducking behind the jewelry display as panic flooded her system.

What was happening right now? How had Cam found her? And why had she just spent the last five minutes mentally undressing him like some kind of desperate woman who hadn't touched a man in months? Which, come to think of it, she hadn't, but still.

"You feelin' alright?" asked the vendor, leaning forward with concern.

"Yes, I'm fine..." January peered around the display,

straining to get a better look. Yep, there was Cam, now examining what looked like a woven bracelet with his paper bag of food tucked under one arm, still looking unfairly attractive in the Caribbean sunlight.

She'd turned off her phone yesterday after that guilt-inducing call with her mother and enduring Brenda's increasingly worried voice asking why she was staying away over the holidays.

But now, staring at Cam across the crowded market, the pieces clicked into place with clarity. Her mother knew exactly where she was.

Of course she'd call Cam. The one person January trusted completely, the one person who might actually be able to talk her into coming home.

January watched as Cam paid for something, the bracelet, she assumed, and tucked it into his pocket. He was probably hungry, had come for food, and was being typical Cam; efficient, buying a gift for one of his family members.

The thought made her chest tighten.

He glanced around the market but not like he was searching for someone. More like he was taking it all in, maybe deciding whether to browse more stalls or head out.

It was terrifying. Because if Cam was here, it meant her escape was over. It meant facing everything she'd run from; her mother's expectations, those mysterious birthday plans, the reality of her unemployment, and apparently, feelings for her best friend that were decidedly not professional.

"Thank you," she said quickly to the jewelry vendor, not buying anything, and started moving through the crowd in the opposite direction from Cam. She needed to get back to Sea La Vie, needed to think, needed to figure out how to handle this without completely falling apart.

But as she wove between families browsing Christmas

decorations and couples sharing plates of flying fish, January couldn't shake the image of Cam in that white linen shirt. Or stop her traitorous brain from replaying the way her body had reacted to seeing him before she'd realized who he was.

Three years of working together, of carefully maintained professional boundaries, of telling herself that she didn't date coworkers for very good reasons. And it had taken one glimpse of him in vacation clothes with his forearms exposed in a foreign country for her to realize that maybe her feelings for Cameron Carter weren't quite as platonic as she'd convinced herself they were.

Nope.

She shook her head. She wasn't dealing with any of that right now.

By six o'clock that evening, January was still processing the reality of seeing Cam at the Christmas market. She'd spent the afternoon helping Jianna arrange flowers for Christmas dinner, but her hands moved on autopilot while her mind replayed that moment of recognition—and the mortifying minutes before it when she'd been admiring his body like some kind of romance novel heroine.

She'd tried to distract herself by unpacking the few things she'd bought at the market, by taking a long shower, by attempting to read on her balcony. Nothing worked. Every time she closed her eyes, she saw Cam in that linen shirt, shopping for food and gifts like he had all the time in the world. Like he belonged here.

For her? Was the gift for her?

He'd come all the way to Barbados. For her.

The weight of that realization sat heavy in her chest.

"Right then, ladies," Cheryl announced, appearing on the terrace with a pitcher of a red concoction. "Happy hour time. Who wants a rum punch made from Bajan rum?"

January raised her glass of lemonade, ready to taste the famous drink, as Kelsi and Monica cheered. She'd gotten to know the two women over the past few days. Monica owned a bookstore in Chicago and was dealing with a broken heart, while Kelsi was a compliance manager from Atlanta who'd needed to escape her hectic life for the holidays.

They'd bonded over breakfast yesterday, all three of them carefully dancing around the real reasons they were hiding in Barbados for Christmas. But sitting here now, with Cam somewhere on the island looking for her, January felt the walls crumbling.

"I wrote in my journal today," Monica said, accepting a glass of punch. "Three whole pages without checking my phone once. That's progress."

"I didn't even bring my laptop to the beach," Kelsi added. "My assistant would have a heart attack if she knew I was this disconnected from email."

January took a sip of her drink, enjoying the smooth, strong rum. "I saw someone I know today. At the Christmas market in Holetown."

Monica looked up from her glass with interest. "Oh? Who was it?"

"My coworker. Well, former coworker." January stared at the ice cubes floating in her drink. "He's here. In Barbados. My mother obviously sent him to find me."

"Your mother sent someone after you?" Kelsi's eyebrows shot up. "Wow. That's...intense."

"It's very much her brand," January said with a sigh. "When Brenda Edwards wants something done, she finds a way to make it happen."

Monica curled up in her chair, regarding January. "So what's the plan? Are you going to talk to him?"

"I...guess, maybe? Eventually." January knew she sounded uncertain even to her own ears and she hated it. "The thing is, seeing him today, it was weird."

"Weird how?" Kelsi asked.

January felt heat crawl up her face. "I kinda didn't recognize him at first. I saw this fine man across the market and I was maybe...appreciating the view." She stared up at the ceiling, not wanting to meet their eyes. "And then he turned around and it was Cam and I wanted to die of embarrassment."

Kelsi chuckled. "You were checking out your coworker?"

"Former coworker," January corrected automatically. "And yes, apparently. Which is mortifying because I've spent three years telling myself we were just friends."

"Question," Monica said gently, "Do any of your other male friends inspire that kind of reaction?"

"No," January admitted. "But that's the problem. What if I've been lying to myself this whole time? What if the reason none of my relationships worked out is because I was already hung up on someone else?"

"Is that such a terrible thing to discover about yourself?" Kelsi asked.

January stared into her drink. "It is when that someone is your best friend and you might completely destroy the relationship by admitting it."

"You think he'd stop being your friend if he knew you were attracted to him?" Monica asked.

"I don't know. Maybe. Or maybe things would just get weird and awkward and we'd lose what we have." January's voice grew smaller. "Cam is...he's the best part of my work life. Was the best part. He's the person I trusted most, who always had my back, who made even the worst days bearable. What if I ruin that?"

"What if you don't?" Kelsi countered gently.

"But what if I do?" January looked up at them, hating how vulnerable she sounded. "And even if I didn't ruin it, the timing is terrible. I just lost my job, I'm having some kind of midlife crisis in a foreign country, I don't even know who I am when I'm not defined by my work. This is probably the worst possible time to suddenly realize I have feelings for someone."

Monica shrugged. "Or maybe it's the perfect time. When else are you going to have the space to figure out how you really feel about him?"

"When I'm not a complete mess," January said. "When I have my life together. When I can offer him something other than chaos and unemployment."

"I don't know him, but I am pretty sure he doesn't care about any of that," Kelsi said matter-of-factly. "If he flew to Barbados to check on you, I bet he's not worried about your employment status."

January sighed deeply. "That's what makes it worse. He's this amazing, supportive friend who would probably be understanding about the whole thing, and I'm too scared to risk losing that friendship by wanting more."

"So what's the alternative?" Monica asked. "You avoid him forever?"

"I don't know." January looked out at the sunset. "I'm sure he's worried about me and he's dealing with my mother, who can be relentless when she wants something."

January took another sip of her punch, feeling the rum warm her from the inside out. "I should probably talk to him."

Monica leaned forward. "You came here because you wanted to stop making safe choices, right? You wanted to figure out who you are when you're not playing it safe all the time."

January was quiet for a long moment, watching the waves roll onto the beach below. "I'm scared," she finally admitted. "What if I tell him how I feel and it ruins everything? What if he doesn't feel the same way? What if he does but then we try dating and it's a disaster and I lose my best friend?"

"Yes, that could happen...but, what if it's wonderful?" Monica asked simply.

"I don't know if I'm brave enough to find out," January said quietly, hating how vulnerable she sounded.

Kelsi raised her glass. "Then maybe that's what you figure out while you're here. Whether you're brave enough to risk something good for the chance at something amazing."

"He's probably staying somewhere nearby," January said finally, pulling out her phone. She'd turned it back on after getting back from the market, and sure enough, there were three missed calls from Cam and two texts.

> CAM: I'm in Barbados. Your mom's worried, but I told her I'd just make sure you're okay. Can we talk?

> I promise I'm not here to drag you home.

Her finger hovered over his contact. She could call him. Should call him. He'd come all this way, and she owed him at least a conversation.

But what would she say? "Hey, sorry I ran away from you at the market after mentally undressing you like some kind of desperate woman?"

"Most likely," Monica agreed, watching January stare at her phone. "The question is...do you want to be found?"

January looked at Cam's texts again. He wasn't here as her mother's messenger. He was here because he cared.

Before she could overthink it, January pressed the call button.

Chapter Six

Cam

Cam stared at the ceiling of his ridiculously overpriced hotel room, on the phone with Brenda Edwards as she tried to help him track down her daughter.

It was Christmas Eve afternoon, and he'd been in Barbados for less than twelve hours. The morning had been a blur—landing at Grantley Adams, the chartered ride to Sandy Lane, checking into a hotel room that cost more per night than his mortgage payment. He'd barely dropped his bags before heading out to search.

He'd walked Holetown's main strip, his jet-lagged brain trying to formulate a plan.

The Christmas market had seemed like a good place to start—lots of locals and tourists, so someone might know about SisterStay properties. Plus, he'd been starving. He'd bought fried flying fish and ate it standing up while browsing craft stalls, hoping to spot January or at least find something to bring her when he found her. The woven bracelet in his pocket now felt like a small, inadequate gesture.

But January was nowhere to be seen. The island had swallowed her whole.

"I've been thinking about where January might be staying," Brenda said. "She mentioned something about an app for women traveling alone. Sister-something? I should have paid more attention."

"SisterStay?" Cam sat up straighter. He'd heard of it—a platform for solo female travelers to find safe accommodations with vetted female hosts.

"Yes, I believe that's it. SisterStay. She said it was like Airbnb but specifically for women who are traveling alone. Safer, you know?" Brenda's voice carried a mix of relief and worry. "At least I know she's somewhere safe, but Cameron, I wish she was here. January always handles all the technology for our family video calls and without her, it's going to be chaos."

"I can help you with that once I find her," Cam said, already pulling up the SisterStay app on his phone. "Let me see what properties they have in Barbados."

"You'd do that? Oh, thank goodness. When you bring her home, you're both coming over for Sunday dinner. I'll make my famous mac and cheese—the kind with three different cheeses, not that boxed stuff."

Cam scrolled through the SisterStay listings, looking for properties that might appeal to January. "Miss Brenda, I need to—"

His phone lit up with an incoming call. He nearly dropped the device when she saw the name on the display.

January.

"Miss Brenda, it's January...I need to go. I'll call you back later."

"Tell her she needs to come home, Cam."

"I'll call you back," Cam said, switching to the other line before she hung up.

"January?"

"Hey, Cam."

He waited, forcing himself not to throw a million questions at her.

"I know you're here in Barbados...I'm assuming my mother sent you?"

Cam's heart hammered against his ribs. She sounded calm, not angry, which was a good thing. "Well, she did ask me to come. She's worried about you, you know?"

He heard January sigh. "I told her I wasn't going to be home for Christmas or my birthday and she freaked, I guess."

"Pretty much."

"But you're okay?" Cam couldn't keep the concern from his voice.

"I'm good. I booked this trip on a whim, but I needed this." A pause. "How long have you been here?"

"Just got in this morning." Cam swung his legs over the side of the bed, feet landing on the plush hotel carpet. "You could have said something..."

He wanted to say he was worried sick and he missed her, but he held back, not wanting to scare her off.

"I know...I just... I needed to get away."

Her voice carried that familiar note of guilt that always made his chest tighten. "And now you're here."

Another pause and Cam waited, knowing she needed to process.

"Cam, where are you staying?"

"This fancy place called Sandy Lane? You heard of it?"

"Oh wow...yeah, I've heard of it. Golf course and penthouse

suites, right?" January sounded impressed. "You must be getting a nice holiday bonus."

Normally, bonuses for profitable years were paid in January, but with the layoffs, Cam doubted they'd get anything come the new year.

"This was all my cousin could find," he said, as he glanced at the opulent furnishings of his room, feeling slightly ridiculous among all the luxury. "I feel like I should take my shoes off when I enter my room."

A soft laugh came through the phone, and Cam closed his eyes for a moment, savoring the sound.

God, he'd missed her laugh.

"So," January said, her voice turning practical, "should we meet up? You did fly all this way to find me. I guess you should give Brenda a full report."

"I'll tell her you're still in one piece, assuming you are when I see you, but I'm here because I was worried about you." He kept his voice casual.

A beat of silence hung between them.

"There's a place called The Tides in Holetown," January said finally. "It's right on the beach, casual. Can you meet me there in an hour?"

"Yes. Absolutely." Cam was already reaching for his shoes. "I'll be there."

"Hey, Cam?"

"Yeah?"

"Thanks for coming. Even if my mother did guilt you into it."

After she hung up, Cam sat on the edge of his massive hotel bed, staring out at the ocean. In an hour, he'd see January for the first time since she'd walked out of PeachTech with that cardboard box and her shoulders held straight despite everything falling apart.

He'd spent the entire flight telling himself this was about helping Brenda, about being a good friend, about making sure January was safe. But sitting in his overpriced paradise, getting ready to see the woman he'd been quietly in love with for three years, Cam finally admitted the truth to himself.

He hadn't flown to Barbados to convince January to come home for a surprise party she didn't even know about.

He'd come because the thought of her being so hurt she'd had to run off alone somewhere was unbearable. He'd come because missing her felt like losing a piece of himself. He'd come because January Edwards wasn't just his closest friend and former work partner.

She was the most important person in his world, and he'd follow her anywhere to make sure she was okay.

Even if she never felt the same way about him.

Cam stood up and walked to his suitcase, suddenly aware that he had no idea what to wear to meet January at a casual beach bar. He'd packed mostly business casual clothes: khakis, button-downs, one pair of dress shoes that were completely wrong for sand. The white linen shirt he'd worn to the market earlier was wrinkled and slightly damp with sweat from walking in the midday heat.

He settled on clean khakis and a black polo shirt, then caught himself checking his reflection in the bathroom mirror. When had he started caring what he looked like around January? They'd worked together for three years, seen each other during flu season and after all-nighters debugging code. She'd seen him at his worst.

But this was different. This wasn't the office. This was a Caribbean beach bar at sunset, and he was about to have a conversation that could change everything between them.

The evening air was perfect as Cam walked the fifteen minutes from Sandy Lane to Holetown. The temperature had cooled to that ideal point where you barely noticed it, and a gentle breeze carried the scent of frangipani and salt air. He passed other resorts catching glimpses of couples sitting on verandas with rum punches.

It struck him that this was the first time since arriving in Barbados that he wasn't frantically searching for January or stressing about the surprise party. For these few minutes, he was just a guy walking to meet someone important to him on a beautiful Caribbean evening.

The Tides turned out to be exactly what January had promised—a casual open-air bar with weathered wooden tables and chairs scattered across a deck that extended almost to the sand. Reggae music drifted from speakers hidden among palm trees, and he could smell grilled fish and rum in the air.

Cam ordered a rum and Coke from the bartender, a woman with shoulder length locs and the warmest smile he'd seen since arriving in Barbados. "You waiting for someone special?" she asked, sliding the drink toward him with a knowing look.

"My friend is meeting me here," Cam said, though the word 'friend' felt inadequate. "She's staying on the island."

"Good luck," she added with a wink that made Cam wonder if he was being more obvious than he thought.

He chose a table with a clear view of the entrance, positioning himself so he could see January when she arrived. The sun was beginning its descent toward the horizon, painting the sky in shades of orange and pink that no Atlanta sunset could match.

Other patrons filtered in. Everyone seemed relaxed in that way that only happened in places where the ocean was always visible and time moved differently.

Cam checked his phone. Still ten minutes until January was supposed to arrive, but he found himself scanning every woman who walked up the beach path. His pulse jumped each time he saw someone with January's build or hair color, only to settle back to normal when it turned out to be a stranger.

January was walking up the path from the beach, and Cam's breath caught in his throat. She was wearing a simple white sundress that skimmed just above her knees, the fabric flowing with each step. Her dark brown skin had taken on a golden glow from the Caribbean sun, and her shoulder-length black hair was loose and wavy around her face instead of pulled back in her usual professional low ponytail. She looked relaxed in a way he'd never seen before.

This was the first time Cam had really seen January truly outside of their work context, and the difference was striking. At PeachTech, she'd always been polished and controlled, her expressive dark eyes focused and serious behind her glasses. Now, without the weight of corporate expectations, her natural beauty was shining through, and he appreciated it even more.

January was nearly five-foot-seven, with curves that her work blazers had always kept professional and understated. The strapless sundress revealed elegant shoulders and arms that looked stronger than he'd imagined, probably from whatever activities she'd been doing since arriving in Barbados.

But it was her face that really caught him off guard. January had always been beautiful, but there was something different about her now. The tension lines around her eyes had softened, and there was a peacefulness to her expression that he hadn't seen in the three years they'd worked together. She looked like herself, but more like someone who'd finally given herself permission to breathe.

She spotted him and raised her hand in a small wave, a tentative smile crossing her full lips. As she walked toward his table, Cam realized that everything was about to change between them.

He just hoped they'd both survive it.

Chapter Seven

January

January's palms were sweating as she walked the beach path toward The Tides, and it had nothing to do with the warm Caribbean evening. She'd spent an hour getting ready. Not for a date, but for Cam. The distinction felt important even if she wasn't entirely sure why.

The white cotton dress had won out in the end, simple and unassuming. She didn't want to look like she'd tried too hard, even though she absolutely had.

The past few days at Sea La Vie had changed something in her. She was not the same January Edwards who'd sat in that Atlanta conference room getting fired five days ago. This January had spent her morning mentoring Jianna about making the most of her internship with Cheryl, her afternoon bonding with Monica and Kelsi over rum punch, and her evening deciding to face the man she'd been avoiding thinking about for three years.

As The Tides came into view, January spotted Cam

immediately. He was sitting at a table near the edge of the deck, a glass in front of him, his attention focused on the ocean. Even from a distance, she could see the tension in his shoulders and the urge to rub the stress out of them gripped her. This was the same posture he got during difficult product meetings when he was trying to solve a particularly complex problem.

Except this time, she imagined she was the problem he was trying to solve.

He looked so good. The black polo shirt emphasized his broad shoulders, and she could see the definition of his arms where the sleeves ended. January's stomach did a strange flip.

He was the same man she'd worked beside for three years, but seeing him here, in this setting, without the buffer of professional boundaries between them, made her pulse quicken in a way that had nothing to do with nerves.

When he spotted her and stood up, offering that familiar half smile that had gotten her through countless stressful workdays, January's carefully constructed walls wobbled.

"Well, well," she said, as she approached the table, one eyebrow raised. "Look what the Christmas Eve tide washed up."

"Hey, Merry Christmas Eve to you too," Cam replied, giving her a grin that she felt all the way to her toes. "See you still got your sense of humor."

"You know me. I just save it for people who don't track me down like I'm a missing person."

January took the chair across from him, unable to suppress her own smile. "Seriously, Cam. You flew to Barbados on Christmas Eve? That's either really sweet or really stalkerish."

"Definitely leaning toward stalkerish," Cam said, settling back into his chair. "But blame your mother. This was initially her idea."

"Of course it was." January rolled her eyes. "Let me guess. She played the worried mother card and you couldn't say no."

"Something like that. You know I can't resist your mother. And she promised me a huge Sunday dinner when we get back. She knows the way to my heart is through my stomach."

He patted his flat abs and January's gaze lingered way longer than it should have. When had he gotten so...defined? She forced herself to look away before he caught her staring.

January nodded in acknowledgment. "I get it. She shows her love through feeding people and you're practically family anyway. And her mac and cheese is the truth."

"That's what she said. Three different cheeses, apparently." Cam signaled the server.

"So what kind of girly, fruity concoction are you drinking tonight? I'm betting something with at least three tropical fruits and an umbrella."

"That obvious, huh?" January settled back in her chair and picked up the menu, grateful for the distraction. "I'll take a Passiontini. I've been drinking rum punch most of the day."

"Most of the day?" Cam raised an eyebrow, his expression shifting to one of amused concern. "Damn, I was thinking island life was just agreeing with you. That's just liquor glow."

"There's a difference between liquor glow and vacation glow," January replied, feeling heat rush to her cheeks that had nothing to do with her day drinking. "I've had exactly two drinks today, thank you very much."

Cam leaned forward, studying her face with an intensity that made her heart beat faster. She fought the urge to smooth her hair or check if her lipstick was still in place.

"Well, whatever it is, it looks good on you," he said, his voice dropping slightly.

"Thank you." January settled into her chair, hyperaware of

the way his gaze lingered on her. "You clean up pretty well yourself. Very tropical resort chic."

"I feel like I'm playing dress-up," Cam admitted, gesturing to his outfit. "Sandy Lane has a dress code for everything. I had to Google what 'resort casual' meant."

"Poor baby," January teased, falling back into their familiar dynamic. "How will you survive in paradise?"

Cam laughed, and January felt the sound ripple through her in a way that was entirely new and disconcerting. Had his laugh always been this warm, this magnetic?

"I think I'll survive," he said, his eyes crinkling at the corners. "It'll be rough, but I'll power through."

January smirked. "I can't imagine how staying at one of the most exclusive resorts on this island will be rough but okay."

"I mean, don't get me wrong, it's beautiful, but I feel out of place." Cam's expression grew more serious. "Kind of like how I felt when I realized my best friend had left the country without telling me."

There it was. The real reason they were both here.

"I'm sorry." January took a deep breath. "I know I should have called you, should have explained what I was doing. I just, I needed to do this on my own."

"I get that. I do. But I was worried about you after that shit went down at work. You gave me some vague answers via text and I'm wondering if you're okay then I find out from your mother that you're sipping cocktails on a beach in Barbados."

The hurt in his voice made her wince, and she started to defend herself, but she let him have his say.

"You've never just vanished before. Even when that asshole Devon with the fake rap career broke up with you via text, you still called me back."

January flinched slightly. Devon had been a mistake in a

long line of dating mistakes with men who hadn't made her feel the way Cam was making her feel right now just by being worried about her.

"This was different," she said quietly. "Losing my job...it wasn't just about the job. It made me realize how small my life had become. Work, sleep, work, sleep, maybe a date with someone I was never going to love. I needed to figure out who I am when I'm not trying to be the perfect employee."

"And who are you?"

January looked out at the ocean, where the sun was painting the water in shades of gold and coral. "I don't know yet. But I'm starting to figure it out."

A comfortable silence fell between them, broken only by the sound of waves and distant reggae music. The server, a young man with a warm smile, approached their table.

"What can I get for you?"

Cam ordered her Passiontini and another rum and Coke.

When the server left, she turned back to Cam. "So my mother sent you."

"She's frantic. Something about Christmas Eve video calls and technology she can't figure out." Cam's mouth twitched into a smile. "I may have promised to help her with her computer when we get back."

"We?"

The question hung between them, heavier than it should have been.

"I meant when I get back," Cam corrected quickly. "I'm not here to drag you home, January. Your mom asked me to try, but I reminded her you're an adult who can make her own decisions."

"Then why are you here?"

Cam was quiet for a long moment, tapping his fingers

against his empty glass. "Because the thought of you being upset and alone somewhere was killing me. Because I've missed you every single day since you left. Because I needed to make sure you were okay."

January raised a hand to her mouth. In three years of friendship, Cam had never said anything like that to her. They'd been close, sure, but always within the safe boundaries of workplace relationships and her own carefully maintained rules.

"Cam..."

"I know. I know we've never talked like this before. But we don't work together anymore, so maybe we can be honest about some things."

Their drinks arrived, giving her a moment to process his words. When she looked up, Cam was watching her with an intensity she'd never seen from him before.

"Like what?" she asked, holding her breath.

"Like the fact that I've been in love with you for three years," Cam said quietly. "And that seeing you walk up that path tonight in that dress nearly stopped my heart."

January stared at him, her mind reeling. "You...what?"

"I'm in love with you, January. I have been since about six months after we started working together. I just never said anything because you made it clear that workplace relationships were off-limits, and I didn't want to lose what we had."

"But we don't work together anymore," she said, her voice barely above a whisper.

"No. We don't."

The air between them crackled with possibility. January took a long sip of her drink, the sweet liquid doing nothing to calm her racing pulse. Everything she thought she knew about their relationship was reshaping itself in real time.

"I saw you at the Christmas market this morning," she said suddenly.

Cam's eyebrows rose. "You did?"

"I didn't recognize you at first." January felt heat flood her cheeks. "I saw this really attractive guy in khakis and a white shirt, and I was very into it. And then you turned around and it was you, and I wanted to die of embarrassment."

A slow smirk spread across Cam's face. "You were checking your boy out?"

"Uh, yeah, apparently. Which was mortifying because I'd spent three years telling myself we were just friends." January laughed shakily. "Turns out I might have been lying to myself about that."

"So what does that mean?"

January took a moment to really look at him. The way the evening light played across his features, the way his eyes had never left her face, the way he was leaning slightly forward like he was afraid she might disappear again.

This was Cam. Her Cam. The person who brought her coffee when she was stressed, who stayed late to help her debug impossible problems, who made her laugh during the worst meetings. The person who'd flown across the ocean because he was worried about her.

The person who'd just told her he loved her.

"It means," January said, standing up from her chair, "maybe we should get out of here."

Cam's eyes darkened. "Where did you have in mind?"

"You said your room at Sandy Lane has an ocean view?"

"It does."

"Then show me."

Cam stood so quickly he nearly knocked over his chair. He threw some bills on the table and took January's hand. "It's about a fifteen-minute walk along the beach."

"Perfect," January said, slipping her hand into the crook of his elbow. "That'll give us time to figure out what the hell we're doing."

Chapter Eight

January

The walk back to Sandy Lane felt both eternal and too short. January was hyperaware of everything: the warm sand beneath her sandals, the sound of waves lapping at the shore, the way Cam's hand felt solid and reassuring in hers. They walked in comfortable silence for most of the way and January found herself enjoying the moment.

"Jay," Cam said, as they approached the resort.

"Yeah?"

"I need you to know that I don't have any expectations about tonight. If you just want to talk, or if you change your mind—"

January stopped walking and turned to face him, placing her hand on his chest. "Cam. I'm a grown woman. If I didn't want to be here with you, I wouldn't be."

He covered her hand with his, pressing it against his heart. She could feel it beating rapidly beneath her palm. "I just don't want you to think I followed you to Barbados expecting anything to happen between us."

"But you hoped something would?"

"I mean...I'd be lying if I said I didn't," Cam admitted with a shrug. The moonlight caught in his eyes, reflecting vulnerability January had never seen before.

She stood on her tiptoes and kissed him softly, tasting the rum and possibility on his lips. When she pulled back, his eyes were dark with want.

The elevator ride to his floor was charged with electricity. Every accidental touch, every shared glance built the tension between them. January found herself studying Cam's profile in the elevator's soft lighting, marveling at how different he looked from the man she'd worked beside for years. This version of him—relaxed, determined, vulnerable—was intoxicating.

Cam's hands shook slightly as he slid the key card into his hotel room door. January stood close behind him, close enough that she could smell his cologne mixed with salt air from their beach walk.

"You having second thoughts?" she asked softly, recognizing his nervousness.

"No...not about this." He pushed open the door and turned to face her. "Are you?"

She started to say something light to keep the moment on the surface, but she realized she couldn't. He'd been nothing but real with her this evening and he deserved the same. January stepped closer, close enough that she had to tilt her head back to meet his eyes. "I've never been more sure of anything in my life."

"Even though it changes everything between us?"

"Especially because it changes everything." Her hand came up to rest against his chest, right over his heart. "I'm tired of being careful, Cam. I'm tired of making safe choices that avoid risk but don't actually make me happy."

He cupped her face in his hands, his thumbs stroking along her cheekbones. "I've wanted this...you...for so long."

"Then stop talking and kiss me."

When his lips met hers, January melted into his touch, returning his kiss with a hunger she had never felt before. Cam pulled her close, one hand splayed across her lower back, pressing her against the hard planes of his chest. She could feel his heart racing, his arousal evident against her stomach. Cam picked her up, cradling her in his arms like she weighed nothing. He kicked the door shut with his foot and carried her toward the balcony doors.

"We giving anyone a free show?" She whispered against his ear.

"Nope, this is the top floor. Your virtue is safe."

He set her down on the railing and she looped her arms around his neck. "I want you, Cam."

His response was to slide his hands under her dress and lifted her slightly, bringing her face level with his. The ocean breeze wrapped around them both, carrying the scent of hibiscus from the resort gardens below.

"God, you feel so good."

Cam's touch was reverent, exploratory, as if he were memorizing every inch of her skin. His fingers traced patterns along her thighs that made her breath catch. She could see in his eyes that he was fighting for control, wanting to savor this moment they'd both imagined but never dared to hope for.

Her dress was bunched at her waist, and she lifted it above her head, tossing it aside. The cotton fabric fluttered to the balcony floor, leaving her in nothing but her black panties. Cam's sharp intake of breath made her feel powerful, desired in a way she'd never experienced before.

Cam immediately went to work, taking one nipple into his mouth. January let out a soft moan against the balcony railing as he teased and suckled, alternating between her breasts. His hands slid down her sides to cup her ass, lifting her closer to his mouth.

"Cam..." she pleaded as his mouth traveled down her body to her stomach, planting soft kisses along the way. "You're overdressed..."

She tugged impatiently at his polo shirt, and he pulled away just long enough to yank it over his head. January sighed happily at the sight of his bare chest, all defined muscle and smooth brown skin that she'd fantasized about earlier.

"Better?" he asked, his voice husky with desire.

"Much," she whispered, running her hands across his shoulders and down his chest.

Cam stepped out of his shorts and kicked them aside, standing before her completely naked. A shiver ran down her spine at the sight. "Damn, Clayton," she breathed. His smile was slow and wicked as he slid his hands between their bodies, tracing the edge of her panties. The anticipation of his touch had her body humming with need.

"I want to take my time with you," he murmured against her neck, his breath hot against her skin. "I've imagined this so many times, but I want to do this right."

"Did you imagine us in Barbados on a balcony on Christmas Eve?"

"No," Cam admitted with a low chuckle, his fingers hooking into the waistband of her panties. "In my fantasies, we were usually in that conference room on our floor after everyone had gone home." He paused, his eyes meeting hers. "This is so much better than anything I imagined."

January lifted her hips, allowing him to slide the black

panties down her legs. The ocean breeze kissed her heated skin, making her shiver with anticipation rather than cold.

"And here I thought the beach would be my most exhilarating experience in Barbados," January whispered as Cam lowered his mouth to her inner thigh.

The ocean breeze caressed their naked bodies as Cam knelt before her, his hands gripping her hips to steady her against the railing. January gasped as his mouth found her center, and she ran frantic fingers over his head. The sensation of his tongue against her most sensitive spot made her legs tremble.

"Oh my God," she whispered, her head falling back as she gazed at the stars above. The Bajan night sky seemed to pulse in rhythm with her heartbeat as Cam's skilled mouth brought her closer to the edge. January wanted to hold on to the moment. She was in Barbados, and her best friend was loving her down like her body was made just for him. She clutched the railing with one hand as her hips began to move against his mouth.

"Cam," she gasped. "I need you. Like right now."

He rose to his feet, his eyes never leaving hers as he reached into his discarded shorts pocket and pulled out a condom. She smirked. Cam was always prepared for any and all contingencies. Taking the package from him, she tore it open with her teeth and rolled it onto him with a quickness.

Cam lifted her from the railing, his arms wrapping around her waist as she guided him inside her. Their mouths met in a heated kiss as they moved together in perfect rhythm

"You feel amazing," Cam whispered against her neck, his voice hoarse with emotion.

January responded by tightening her grip on his shoulders, her fingernails leaving crescent marks on his skin. "So do you..."

She pressed her forehead against his, her lips parting in a strangled cry as her body tensed. Cam's movements became more urgent, his hands gripping her hips tightly as he followed her over the edge, whispering her name.

For several moments, they remained locked together, their bodies trembling.

"That was..." she said, then shook her head. "I don't have words."

"What...I've rendered January Edwards speechless...who knew that was even possible," he was grinning at her now like the cat who ate the canary. "I should probably get a Noble Prize or something, right?"

She swatted at him. "Let's go inside. It's a little chilly out here."

Cam swept her up again, carrying her through the sliding glass doors into the air-conditioned suite. He placed her on the bed as January took in the spacious room and king-sized bed. "You weren't kidding about this place. This is amazing."

He scooped up their clothes from the balcony and deposited them onto a chair near the bed. "Told you."

Cam walked to the side of the bed and sat down next to January. "I'm just glad you called me. I wasn't sure how I was going to track you down."

"You would have figured something out." January reached for his hand, intertwining her fingers with his. "Though I'm still mad at my mother for sending you."

"Are you really?" Cam raised an eyebrow.

January's lips curved into a smile. "Nope. But don't tell her that."

Chapter Nine

Cam

Cam woke to unfamiliar warmth pressed against his side and the sound of waves outside his window. For a moment, he lay perfectly still, afraid that moving would somehow break the spell of the night before. January was curled against him, her dark hair spread across his shoulder, one hand resting over his heart.

The morning light filtering through the balcony doors painted everything in gold, making the whole scene feel like something out of a dream. Except it wasn't a dream. January Edwards—his January—was actually here, in his bed, wearing nothing but one of his tee shirts on Christmas morning. Not exactly how he'd pictured this holiday turning out, but he wasn't complaining.

"Morning," she murmured against his shoulder, her voice husky with sleep.

Relief flooded through him at the contentment in her tone. "Morning." He pressed a gentle kiss to the top of her head, breathing in the scent of her coconut-scented hair. "Merry Christmas."

January's eyes flew open. "Oh my God, it's Christmas. I completely forgot." She sat up slightly, looking adorable and disheveled in his oversized tee shirt. "Merry Christmas."

"You okay?"

January was quiet for a moment, and Cam's chest tightened with worry. Then she lifted her head to look at him with a slightly mischievous expression that made his heart skip. "Well, I definitely understand why Sandy Lane charges so much now. This bed is incredible," she ran a hand over her pillow. "These sheets are the softest I've ever felt."

Cam laughed, the sound rumbling through his chest as tension he hadn't realized he was carrying melted away. "That's your biggest takeaway from last night? The thread count?"

"I'm a product manager, Cam. I notice quality when I experience it." January's eyes lit up with amusement. "Five stars across all metrics."

"All metrics?" Cam raised an eyebrow, grinning down at her. The fact that she was teasing him, that she seemed genuinely happy, made something warm unfurl in his chest.

"Mmm," January pretended to consider seriously, tapping her finger against his chest in a way that made his skin tingle. "User experience was exceptional. Performance exceeded expectations. Would definitely recommend to...well, never mind that, because I'm keeping this all to myself."

"Possessive already?" Cam teased, his arms tightening around her. The possessive note in her voice thrilled him more than it probably should have.

"You have no idea," January said, then grew more serious. Cam watched her face carefully, reading the emotions that flickered across her features. "I keep expecting to feel guilty or scared or like I've made a terrible mistake. But I don't. I feel..."

she paused, searching for the right word. "Free, I guess. Like I finally did something just because I wanted to, not because it made sense or fit into some plan."

Cam felt his chest expand with something that might have been pure happiness. Three years of careful friendship, of wondering and hoping and never daring to act, had led to this moment. January Edwards—brilliant, cautious, careful January —was lying in his arms talking about feeling free. And he'd been part of giving that to her.

Relief flooded through Cam so intensely he had to close his eyes for a moment. "I was afraid you'd wake up regretting everything."

"Are you serious?" January propped herself up on her elbow, looking down at him with an expression that was part amusement, part lingering desire. "Cam, last night was incredible. You were incredible."

"Damn, you're good for a brotha's ego..." he smirked at her, trying to hide how much her words meant to him. "But I don't know if I can take full credit...there was a lot of pent-up...excitement."

She leaned against his chest and Cam wrapped his arms around her, acutely aware of how perfect she felt there.

"January—" he started, thinking about everything waiting for them back home, but she shifted, straddling him, and his train of thought derailed completely as she leaned down to kiss him. The tee shirt rode up, and his hands automatically went to her thighs.

"Later," she whispered against his lips. "Right now, I just want this."

They made love again, slower this time, with the morning sun streaming through the windows.

Afterward, they lay tangled together, catching their breath.

"I had no idea you were interested in me like that," January said finally. "This is literally the first time you've been single since I started at PeachTech."

"You had that no-dating-coworkers rule. But also, I mean we just clicked when we first met. You were this cool techy woman and I figured we'd be friends and that was it," he shrugged. "Somewhere along the line, I started comparing the women I dated to you and they were falling short."

She was tracing circles with her manicured nail against his thigh and Cam found it increasingly difficult to focus on the conversation.

"Falling short how?" January asked, genuine curiosity in her voice.

Cam caught her hand, stilling its movement before he lost his train of thought entirely and pulled her out of his shirt and on top of him. "They weren't you. They didn't make me laugh the way you do, they didn't challenge me intellectually, didn't get my Archer jokes."

"No one watched that show but you," January snorted.

"Liar," Cam said, grinning. "You watched at least three episodes with me."

January rolled her eyes, but her smile betrayed her. "Only because you fast-tracked that bug fix that I needed." She sighed. "You were always willing to help me out. You did whatever I needed without me having to explain too much or make a case for it."

"That's because we worked well together," Cam said, bringing her wrist to his mouth for a kiss. "I trusted your judgment. You never asked for something unless it was important."

"We were a good team."

"We were," Cam agreed, his thumb stroking along her jawline. "Still could be, in a different way."

"You think this can still work once we're back in Atlanta?

That this isn't just a fancy-ass-resort-in-Barbados kind of thing?"

Cam looked at her seriously, recognizing the vulnerability behind her light tone. Three years of working together had taught him to read between the lines with January, to catch the moments when her confident exterior masked deeper worries.

"January," he said softly, shifting so they were face to face, "I didn't fly to Barbados for a vacation hookup. I came here because I couldn't stand the thought of you being somewhere in the world thinking you were alone."

Her shoulders relaxed at his words, and she leaned against him once more.

"That's what kind of scares me," January admitted quietly. "I've gotten so used to keeping work and personal separate, having these neat little compartments. But you managed wiggle in and live rent free in both spaces somehow."

Cam understood what she meant. Even during their most professional interactions, there had been an undercurrent of something deeper: shared glances during tedious meetings, inside jokes that made conference calls bearable, the way they could communicate entire conversations with just a look across the office.

"You know the dev team started calling us Camuary, right?"

January let out a shocked laugh, her eyes widening. "No they didn't! Oh God, that's embarrassing...and a horrible mashup of our names."

"It was kind of cute, actually," Cam said, grinning at the memory. "Kelly from QA started it after that product launch where we stayed until midnight fixing that database issue. She said we were like an old married couple, finishing each other's sentences."

January covered her face with her hands, but her smile

peeked through her fingers. "And here I was thinking I was being the ultimate professional."

"You were. Professional with a capital P," Cam said, his hands running down her sides. "It's one of the things that attracted me to you: beautiful Black woman in tech, handling business and running shit...I might have looked at you a few times like I wanted to strip you naked slowly, but I respected your boundaries."

January burst into laughter, her whole body shaking against his. "Well, that's wild...so you're telling me everyone on the dev team knew you had a thing for me while I was completely oblivious?"

"Pretty much," Cam replied with a grin. "They're a pretty intuitive team. They make my job easier and I'm thankful for them."

January nodded, her face becoming serious. "I'm going to miss working with them." She turned to him. "Cam, what am I gonna do? I don't have a job to go back to."

He rubbed her back. "That's what we're going to figure out together. You're brilliant, January. Any tech company would be lucky to have you."

"You know what's really scary about all this?" January said quietly. The playfulness from moments before had shifted into something more vulnerable.

Cam sensed the change in her tone immediately. "What's that?"

January was quiet for a long moment, staring out at the ocean through the floor-to-ceiling windows. "I keep thinking about my birthday coming up. In a few days I will be forty." She let out a long breath. "It feels like I've fallen behind in life."

"Fallen behind?"

"I mean, I'm going to be forty, Cam. Forty and unemployed and single...well, maybe not single anymore...but still. When I was younger, I thought by forty I'd have it all: the corner office, maybe a husband, kids, a house with a white picket fence and a dog named something ridiculous like Peanut Butter Patty."

Cam couldn't help but smile at that last part. "Peanut Butter Patty?"

"Don't ask," January said, but she was almost smiling too. "I really loved peanut butter as a kid. Anyway, none of that happened. And now I'm here, hiding in Barbados because I can't face the fact that I've somehow failed at being an adult."

Cam's stomach tightened. He thought about Brenda's surprise party and all the effort she'd put into the event: the fifty people, the deposits, the family flying in from across the country. The party January had no idea about and would probably hate.

He should tell her. Right now.

"January, about your birthday... your mom has been planning something," he started carefully.

"I know," January sighed. "She kept dropping hints about 'special plans.' That's part of why I left. I couldn't handle whatever well-meaning thing she had cooked up while I'm feeling like such a mess."

Cam opened his mouth to tell her it was a surprise party, that Brenda had been planning it for months, that he'd known all along. But the vulnerable look on her face stopped him.

"I'm sure she'll understand if you want something low-key this year," he said instead, hating himself for the cowardice even as the words left his mouth.

But January wasn't listening. "I just feel like such a failure, Cam," she said quietly, her eyes filling with tears.

Cam shifted so he could look at her directly. "Jay, you haven't failed at anything."

"Haven't I?" Her voice cracked slightly. "I got fired right

before Christmas. That really only works out in Hallmark movies."

"Hey." Cam cupped her face gently, forcing her to meet his eyes. "You didn't get fired because you weren't good enough. You know that, right? You got caught up in bullshit corporate politics. Your work was excellent."

"Was it though?" She looked away. "Maybe if I'd been more strategic, more political, better at playing the game. I should have seen this coming."

"No." Cam's voice was firm. "Don't do that to yourself. I worked with you every day. I watched you solve problems other people couldn't even identify. You made everyone around you better at their jobs, including me."

January's eyes filled with tears. "Then why do I feel like such a failure?"

"Because losing your job hurts, especially when work was such a big part of your identity. But January, you're so much more than your job title." Cam brushed a tear from her cheek with his thumb. "You're the person who remembers everyone's coffee order and their kids' names. You made that sterile office feel like a place where people actually cared about each other."

"I just..." January took a shuddering breath. "I thought I had more time to figure things out. To become the person I was supposed to be. And now I'm almost forty and I don't even know who that person is anymore."

Cam pulled her closer, feeling the weight of her vulnerability. "Baby, that's okay. Who says you have to have it all figured out by some arbitrary age?"

"Easy for you to say. You still have a job."

"For now. But January, I've been going through the motions for months. Coming to work, doing my job, going home to my empty apartment to watch Silicon Valley reruns and eat takeout. You know what the highlight of my week was? Those

Tuesday morning meetings when you'd bring coffee for everyone and we'd spend ten minutes just talking before we got down to business."

January looked up at him, surprised. "Really?"

"Really. My life isn't any more figured out than yours is. I just had the luxury of not getting fired to force me to confront it." Cam paused, then decided to be completely honest. "You want to know something? I'm terrified."

"Of what?"

"Of going back to Atlanta without you. Of sitting in that office knowing you're not going to walk through the door. Of falling back into that routine where the best part of my day was stolen glances across a conference room." His voice softened. "I'm terrified that this—us—is too good to be real, and that somehow I'm going to mess it up."

January was quiet for a long moment, processing his words. When she spoke again, her voice was steadier. "What if we're both just scared people who have no idea what we're doing?"

"Then maybe we can figure it out together."

She smiled then, the first genuine smile since the conversation had turned serious. "That sounds terrifying and wonderful at the same time."

"The best things usually do," Cam said, pressing a kiss to her forehead.

"Wait here," he said suddenly, sliding out of bed.

"Where are you going?" January asked, propping herself up on her elbows.

Cam walked to the chair where he'd tossed his khakis yesterday and pulled something from the pocket. "I got you something. Well, technically I got it before I found you." He returned to the bed, holding out the woven bracelet he'd bought at the Christmas market.

"Cam, this is beautiful." January's eyes widened as she took it from him. "When did you—"

"Yesterday morning. At the market." He rubbed the back of his neck. "I was hungry and looking for clues about where you might be, and I saw this and thought of you."

"You bought me a Christmas present while you were searching for me in a foreign country?" January's voice was thick with emotion.

"I wanted to bring you something when I found you. A peace offering, I guess." He helped her fasten the bracelet around her wrist. "Merry Christmas, Jay."

January looked at the bracelet, then at him, tears glistening in her eyes. "I didn't get you anything."

"You called me yesterday. That's all the gift I needed." He pulled her close. "Well, that and last night. And this morning. Yeah, I'm definitely not complaining about Christmas in Barbados."

She laughed through her tears and kissed him softly. "Thank you. I love it."

January settled back against his chest, admiring the bracelet on her wrist, and for a moment they lay in comfortable silence, watching the morning light dance across the water.

"Just...I'm glad you called me yesterday," he said.

She smiled without opening her eyes. "Me too. Best Christmas ever."

Cam held her close, the late morning sun warming them through the balcony doors. In a few days, they'd have to go back to Atlanta. Back to reality. Back to everything they'd left behind.

But right now, in this moment, it was just the two of them and the promise of something new.

Chapter Ten

January

January woke to unfamiliar warmth and the sound of waves outside the window. For a moment, she lay still, remembering where she was: Sandy Lane, Cam's hotel room, the morning after Christmas.

The morning after everything had changed between them.

She glanced at Cam sleeping beside her, his face peaceful in the early morning light. Yesterday had been perfect—the bracelet, the intimate conversations, the feeling that maybe, just maybe, she was exactly where she was supposed to be.

Boxing Day in Barbados. She'd never spent the day after Christmas anywhere but Atlanta, and certainly never waking up in a man's bed feeling this content.

Careful not to wake him, January slipped out of bed and padded to the bathroom. The shower felt amazing, the hot water washing away the last remnants of sleep. She stood under the spray, letting her mind wander to Cheryl's villa, to the possibility of spending more time in Barbados, to what a future with Cam might actually look like.

When she turned off the water and wrapped herself in one of Sandy Lane's impossibly soft towels, she heard movement in the bedroom—Cam was awake.

Then she heard his phone ring.

Through the bathroom door, she heard Cam's voice: "Hey, Miss Brenda..."

January opened the bathroom door slightly, about to call out and ask Cam where he'd put her overnight bag, when she heard his footsteps moving toward the balcony.

"Yeah, she's good... No, I haven't talked to her about coming home yet..."

January stood frozen in the bathroom doorway, towel clutched around her, listening as Cam's voice drifted in from the balcony. Through the open balcony door, she could hear Cam clearly.

"Miss Brenda, I don't know if now's the right time to—"

Her mother's voice was loud enough that January could make out the words even from where she stood: "Cameron, the party is in nine days. People are starting to ask questions!"

Party? What party?

January's stomach dropped.

"I know, I know," Cam was saying, his voice strained. "But she's been pretty clear about not wanting a big fuss for her birthday—"

"That's exactly why it needs to be a surprise!" Brenda's voice carried clearly through the room. "The caterers need final numbers, and Celeste and Roy are driving down from Tennessee. Cameron, you've got to get her home before the party!"

January's hand gripped the doorframe, her knuckles white.

He knew.

Cam had known about a surprise party this entire time. While she'd been pouring her heart out about dreading her fortieth birthday, about feeling like a failure, he'd been keeping this secret. Helping her mother plan the exact thing January had been trying to escape.

"I understand," Cam said quietly into the phone. "Let me talk to her and—"

January stepped out of the bathroom, still wrapped in the towel, water dripping onto the plush carpet.

"I'll take it," she said, her voice deadly calm.

Cam spun around from the balcony, his eyes widening as he saw her standing there. The guilt on his face told her everything she needed to know.

"January?" he said softly, lowering the phone slightly.

"Give me the phone, Cameron."

The use of his full name made him wince, but he walked back into the room and handed over the device.

January took a deep breath, trying to keep her voice steady. "Hey, Mom."

"January! Oh, thank goodness you're there with Cameron. Listen, sweetheart, I know you're having a nice time in Barbados, but we need to talk about when you're coming home. And you'll need to act like you're surprised—"

"Mom, please." January's voice was calm but firm. "I heard what you were telling Cam about a party. I need you to listen to me very carefully. I never asked for a surprise party, and I don't want one."

The silence on the other end stretched long enough that January wondered if the call had dropped.

"But baby, it's your fortieth birthday. This is a milestone. Why wouldn't you want to celebrate it with the people who love you?"

January glanced at Cam, who was standing rigidly a few

feet away, his hands clenched at his sides. "Mom, you know I don't like being the center of attention. Especially now that I don't have a job. Everyone's going to ask what I'm doing next, and I don't have answers."

"But I've already put down deposits, and people are flying in from out of town. Your cousins will be here—"

"Then you'll need to call them and explain that you planned this without asking me first." January's voice remained steady, but she could feel the anger blooming, directed at her mother, and at the man standing beside her who'd let this happen. "I'm sorry if this disappoints people, but the last thing I want is a big party where I have to pretend to be surprised."

"January Edwards, you are being selfish. We have worked hard and everyone is expecting—"

"Mom, please." January's voice sharpened. "For thirty-nine years I have done exactly what everyone expected of me. I've followed every rule, been the perfect daughter, the perfect student, the perfect employee. And where has that gotten me? Jobless and standing in a hotel room in Barbados having to defend my right to spend my own birthday however I want."

"January, I just don't understand what's gotten into you—"

"Mom, I'm going to stop you there before we both say something we'll regret. I love you, but I need you to respect my decision about my own birthday. I'll call you later."

January ended the call and held the phone out to Cam, her hand trembling slightly. For a moment, they stood in complete silence, the weight of the conversation settling between them like a wall.

"Jay—" Cam started.

"How long has my mother been planning this party?" January asked quietly, still holding his phone.

Cam ran a hand over his head, the gesture she'd always found endearing now making her want to scream. "I don't know...we talked about it when she had that dinner for your dad's birthday, so June?"

"June?" January stared at him in disbelief, setting his phone down on the nightstand with deliberate care. "You've known about this for months and you never thought to mention it? Even after I told you yesterday morning how terrified I am about turning forty?"

"First of all, it's a surprise birthday party...why would I mention it? That's a dick move. And, honestly, I thought maybe it would be different coming from family since you and your family are so close."

"You thought I'd want to be ambushed by fifty people when I'm at the lowest point of my life?" January's grip tightened on the towel as she moved toward her overnight bag on the chair.

"You've worked with me for three years. You know I hate being the center of attention."

"I was trying to help—"

"Help who?" January grabbed the bag and pulled out her aqua floral sundress, her movements sharp and angry. "Because you certainly weren't helping me. You were helping my mother plan something you knew I would hate."

Cam's face crumpled. "I was caught between you and your mom. She was so excited, so sure this would make you happy—"

"And what about what I wanted? Did it occur to either of you to ask me?" January disappeared back into the bathroom, emerging moments later in the sundress. "Cam, I told you things yesterday morning I've never told anyone. About feeling like a failure, about being scared of forty, about not knowing who I am anymore. And this whole time you knew there was a party planned that would force me to face all of that in front of everyone I know?"

"We didn't know you were going to lose your job, January," he said through clenched teeth.

He might have a point there, but she wasn't going to give him the satisfaction.

January started throwing her things into her bag—toiletries from the bathroom counter, her sandals from beside the bed, the tee shirt she'd borrowed from him.

"What are you doing?" Cam moved toward her.

"I'm leaving." January's voice was flat as she zipped the bag with more force than necessary. "I need to go."

Cam moved to block her way, palms up in a gesture of truce. "You don't have to do this. Please, just...can you put the bag down and talk to me like a human being?"

"You flew here supposedly because you were worried about me," she said, tugging her bag over her shoulder. "But really you came to convince me to go home for a party I never wanted. How is that not manipulation?"

"Manipulation? That's bullshit and you know it." Cam stepped closer, his hands outstretched but not touching her. "I came because I couldn't stand the thought of you being hurt and alone somewhere."

"But you weren't going to tell me about the party, were you? You were just going to let me find out when we got back to Atlanta?" January shook her head, feeling sick. She grabbed her phone from the nightstand and shoved it in her bag. "Or maybe you thought after the past two days I'd be so grateful I'd do whatever you wanted."

"Again, that's how surprise parties work...you don't tell the guest of honor beforehand," Cam said, his jaw tight. "And if we're going there...as I recall, you invited yourself to my room on Christmas Eve."

He moved closer to her, stopping inches away. January, refusing to back down, fought the urge to step back.

"If you think these past two days were about me manipulating you into going back home for a party, you don't know shit about me." His voice was low, controlled, but the muscle in his jaw twitched with tension.

The truth was, January didn't think that at all. But anger and embarrassment were swirling through her body, making her lash out at the nearest target. She wanted to take the words back as soon as they left her mouth, but pride kept her silent.

"Is that really what you think of me?" Cam asked, his voice quieter now, and she could hear something breaking in it. "That I'd use what happened between us to manipulate you?"

"I don't know." She exhaled. "Right now it feels like everyone in my life thinks they know what's best for me better than I do. My mother plans a party I don't want, and my... whatever you are... helps her keep it secret."

"I'm your best friend," Cam said quietly. His voice dropped even lower, and she could see fear flickering in his eyes. "I thought after yesterday you knew exactly what I am to you."

January felt the tears welling up in her eyes as his words hit her. The raw honesty in his voice cut through her anger like a knife. She wanted to stay mad, needed to stay mad, but the vulnerability on his face made it impossible. This was Cam— her Cam—who'd laid himself bare before her yesterday.

"I should go..." she faltered, adjusting the bag on her shoulder. "I need some time to think."

Cam nodded slowly, and she could see him wrestling with whether to say more.

But as she moved toward the door, he called out, "Before you go."

She paused, hand on the doorknob.

"Your mother is going to keep calling. She's going to keep pushing about the party. And when you get back to Atlanta, there's going to be fifty people expecting to celebrate you." His voice was quiet but urgent. "You can be angry at me, but your mother has put a lot of effort into your party. You should at least acknowledge her efforts, even if you don't want the party. She's proud of you and wants to see you happy."

January turned back to him, and for a moment they just looked at each other across the expanse of the hotel room.

"What if what I want is something I'm too scared to ask for?" she whispered.

"Then maybe that's exactly what you should ask for," Cam said simply.

January left the room without another word, pulling the door closed behind her with a quiet click that felt louder than a slam.

Chapter Eleven

January

The hammock situated on the side of the villa between two oversized palm trees had been calling to January since the moment she'd first seen it on the SisterStay website. Now, as she lay swaying gently in the afternoon breeze, she understood why. It was the perfect place to fall apart without anyone watching.

She should have been dozing as the waves crashed against the shore, but instead she was fighting tears and beating herself up over her argument with Cam. How had things gone so wrong so fast? Yesterday they couldn't keep their hands off each other, and now, after one call from her mother, January had accused him of manipulating her.

The Sea La Vie car service had brought her back without question—one of Cheryl's vetted drivers who knew better than to make small talk with an obviously upset guest. January had texted Cheryl when she arrived, letting her know she was back but needed some space.

She'd changed out of the aqua sundress into shorts and a baggy tee before escaping to this quiet corner where the ocean sounds could drown out the chaos in her head.

Boxing Day in Barbados was nothing like the day after Christmas in Atlanta.

No returns and exchanges at crowded malls, no post-holiday cleanup with her mother fussing about putting decorations away properly. Just the rhythmic sound of waves and the distant laughter of children playing on the beach. It should have been peaceful.

Instead, January felt like she was drowning.

"What if what I want is something I'm too scared to ask for?"

Her own words kept running through her head on repeat. She'd meant them about Cam, about the possibility of a real relationship, but she could apply them to every aspect of her life right now. Her career, her relationship with her mother, her entire life. When was the last time she'd actually asked for what she wanted instead of going along with what seemed expected?

"You look like someone who could use a pick-me-up."

January opened her eyes to find Cheryl approaching with two glasses of sorrel.

"May I join you?" Cheryl gestured to the wooden chair positioned near the hammock and placed a glass in January's hand.

"Of course," January said, as she attempted to wipe tears from her cheeks. "You do own the place."

"Yes, but this is your sanctuary right now." Cheryl settled into the chair with the easy grace of someone who'd learned to live at a slower Caribbean pace. "Rough day?"

"You could say that." January sipped the deep red drink, savoring the spicy sweetness. "My mother's been planning a surprise birthday party for me, and my...friend has been helping her."

"Ah." Cheryl's expression remained neutral. "And I'm guessing you're not much of a surprise party person."

"Not even a little bit. I hate being the center of attention. Always have." January swirled the drink in her glass. "But apparently everyone thinks they know what's best for me better than I do."

"Sounds frustrating."

"The worst part is, I can't even be completely mad about it. My mother loves me. I'm her only child and she wants to celebrate me." January's voice caught slightly. "But Cam...Cam was caught between us. It's not like there was a good choice for him."

"But you're still angry."

"Yes...furious actually," January admitted. "I'm angry that he let my mother plan something he should know I would hate. But mostly I'm furious at myself."

Cheryl raised an eyebrow. "For what?"

"For expecting him to read my mind. For never actually setting better boundaries with my mother. For running away to Barbados rather than have a difficult conversation."

January pressed the cool glass against her forehead. "For being thirty-nine years old and still expecting other people to fight my battles for me."

"Can I share a story with you?" Cheryl asked eventually.

January nodded.

"I was a corporate lawyer in London for fifteen years. Made partner at thirty-three, had the corner office, the posh designer suits, the works. From the outside, my life looked perfect."

"I feel there's a but coming...what happened?"

"I had a breakdown in a client meeting. Full panic attack, couldn't breathe, had to be carried out of the office." Cheryl's voice was methodical and matter of fact, like she was describing something she'd seen online, but January could sense the woman's lingering pain underneath. "Spent the next six months in therapy trying to figure out why I was so damn miserable when my life was 'perfect'."

"And?"

"Turns out I'd spent so long being what everyone else wanted me to be that I'd forgotten who I actually was. My parents wanted me to be successful, my firm wanted me to be aggressive and ruthless, my friends wanted me to be the ride-or-die. I was so busy being all those things that I never stopped to ask what I wanted."

January's heart pounded as she listened to Cheryl. "So how did you end up here?"

"First I had to learn how to disappoint people." Cheryl smiled ruefully. "Hardest skill I ever had to master. Saying no to my parents when they wanted me to take the promotion. Saying no to friends who wanted me to go out when I needed to stay home. Saying no to clients who wanted me to be available twenty-four seven."

"How did you figure out what you actually wanted?"

"I started small. What did I want for dinner? What did I want to wear? What did I want to do on Saturday afternoon?" Cheryl gestured toward the ocean. "Eventually I worked up to the bigger questions. What kind of life did I want? What made me feel alive?"

January thought about the past few days at Sea La Vie. The conversations with Jianna about the young woman's career path. The easy camaraderie with Monica and Kelsi. The feeling of being able to relax without having to check her phone for work updates. "I think I'm starting to figure that out."

"Good. Because running away only works for so long. Eventually you have to go back and face the music."

January sat up in the hammock. "What if I mess everything up? What if I hurt people I love by asking for what I want?"

Cheryl leaned forward slightly. "January, what's the alternative? Spending the rest of your life being miserable so other people can be comfortable?"

January frowned. When Cheryl put it like that, her plan of action became clear.

Before January could answer, her phone buzzed with a text. She glanced at the screen and her stomach dropped.

> AUNT CELESTE: Ready for your big day! Your uncle and I are driving down from Tennessee. Your mom says it's going to be huge! Can't wait to see you.

"Oh God," January muttered, showing Cheryl the text.

"Ah. The plot thickens."

"My aunt and uncle are driving six hours for this party. My cousins are probably booking flights. My mother has caterers booked..." January felt the familiar panic rising in her chest. "How can I disappoint all these people?"

"How can you not disappoint yourself?"

The question hung in the air like a challenge. January closed her eyes, feeling the hammock sway beneath her. When she opened them, Cheryl was watching her with patient understanding.

"I need to call my mother," January said quietly.

"Do you?"

"Yeah. I need to have the conversation I should have had months ago. I need to tell her what I actually want for my birthday."

"And what's that?"

"Something quiet. Here...not in Atlanta. I want to start my forties somewhere that actually makes me happy, surrounded by people who accept me as I am right now: unemployed, confused, and figuring things out."

"That sounds lovely. We'll get you a cake."

"But I also need to talk to Cam." January's heart hammered as she replayed their argument earlier. "I need to apologize for some of the things I said. And I need to tell him what I'm scared to ask for."

"Which is?"

"A real relationship with him. Not just the fantasy of one, but the messy, complicated, sometimes disappointing reality of two people trying to build something together." January looked out at the ocean, her thoughts coming together. "I want someone who'll fight for me, but I also want to be brave enough to fight for myself."

Cheryl smiled. "Now that sounds like someone who knows what she wants."

"Speaking of asking for what you want," Cheryl said, settling back in her chair, "I have a proposition for you."

January raised an eyebrow. "Really?"

"I've been watching you these past few days. The way you mentored Jianna, how you've been thinking about business strategy, your insights about guest experience." Cheryl paused, studying January's face. "I'm looking to expand Sea La Vie's offerings, and I think you might be exactly the person I need."

"What kind of expansion?"

"Spa products. Locally sourced, sustainably made bath and body products that capture the essence of Barbados. Sea salt scrubs, coconut and lime body oils, that sort of thing." Cheryl rubbed her hands together. "A local woman who's been making these products for her family for decades has created recipes for me. What I don't have is someone who understands product development, marketing, and how to scale a business."

January felt a familiar spark of interest. "That's actually a really smart idea. Guests can take that experience home with them."

"Exactly. And I'll be supporting local suppliers, creating jobs for women in the community, while adding another revenue stream for Sea La Vie." Cheryl leaned forward. "I'm not talking about a traditional employment situation. I'm thinking partnership. You'd help me develop and launch the line, and in return, you'd get equity in the business and the freedom to work from wherever you want."

January's mind shifted with the possibilities. Product positioning, target markets, distribution channels, branding that captured both luxury and authenticity. "How would the manufacturing work?"

"Small batches initially, using local suppliers for ingredients. We could start with online sales to SisterStay guests and expand from there." Cheryl smiled. "You could spend part of your time here in Barbados working on the business, part of your time back in Atlanta. Complete flexibility."

"That sounds amazing." January paused, thinking of the possibilities. "But I should probably figure out my personal life first."

"Of course. But January, this opportunity isn't going anywhere. And sometimes the best way to figure out your personal life is to get clear on your professional goals first."

January looked out at the ocean, imagining splitting her time between this beautiful island and Atlanta, building something meaningful instead of just climbing someone else's corporate ladder.

"Can I think about it?"

"Take all the time you need. But remember what I said about asking for what you want. Sometimes the universe puts exactly what we need right in front of us."

January thought about Cam, probably sitting in his overpriced hotel room regretting this trip. Regretting that he'd revealed his feelings to her. Regretting he'd ever met her.

"I need to figure out if I've ruined the best thing that ever happened to me."

She thought about the job opportunity Cheryl had just offered, about the possibility of building a life that actually fit her instead of trying to squeeze herself into someone else's expectations.

"But regardless of what he may say, I'm going to ask for what I want," she said, swinging her legs out of the hammock.

Chapter Twelve

Cam

Cam walked Sandy Lane beach, staring at his phone. He'd been holding it for the past hour, trying to work up the courage to do something—anything—but every time he started to type a message to January, he deleted it.

The fight with January kept replaying in his head. The way she'd looked at him before she walked out, her face a mixture of anger and disappointment, like she expected better from him.

She had every right to.

For three years, he'd watched January navigate office politics with grace, stand up for junior product team members when management tried to overload them, and diplomatically but firmly shut down bad ideas in meetings. She wasn't afraid to go to bat for her team, and she'd shouldered the weight of the difficult conversations for them.

But when it came to her own life, she'd somehow convinced herself that other people should fight those battles for her. And he'd let her believe it rather than calling her on it.

He sighed as he watched a pair of sandpipers pick at the white sand.

No, that wasn't fair. January owned her part in this mess, but his part was clear: he'd been a coward. When Brenda had called him bubbling with excitement about the surprise party, he'd known that January wouldn't want it. She always deflected when people made a fuss over her birthday, always downplaying it or changing the subject entirely.

And he'd said nothing because disappointing Brenda Edwards felt impossible.

The woman had become like family to him. She sent cute memes on his birthday, invited him to Sunday dinners, asked about his projects at work with genuine interest. When his own parents had moved to Arizona, citing better weather and lower cost of living, Brenda had somehow filled the gap they'd left.

But choosing her feelings over January's hadn't been protecting anyone. It had been taking the easy way out.

Cam looked at his phone again. He didn't even know where January was. She'd said Sea La Vie when she first told him about it, but he'd never gotten the address. He could probably find it online, but what would he do? Show up uninvited after she'd made it clear she needed space?

He pulled up Instagram, hoping for some sign that she was okay.

Her profile loaded, and there it was: a photo posted an hour ago. The hammock he remembered from the SisterStay website, suspended between two palm trees with the ocean visible in the background. The caption read:

"Learning to ask for what I want. Ready for the next chapter."

Cam stared at the photo. She looked peaceful. Or at least, the hammock looked peaceful. But that caption sounded like someone who'd made a decision. Someone who was moving forward.

With or without him.

The thought made his chest tighten with panic. What if she'd already decided he wasn't worth the risk? What if the past two days had been amazing but not enough to overcome his betrayal? What if "next chapter" meant moving on from him entirely?

He'd been so focused on not losing Brenda's affection that he hadn't considered he might lose January. And now, standing on this beach with his phone in his hand and no idea how to fix what he'd broken, Cam realized that was his pattern.

Avoiding difficult conversations. Choosing comfort over courage. Letting things happen instead of making them happen.

It's what he'd done with January for three years. Watching her date other men, never telling her how he felt because it was easier to maintain the friendship than risk rejection. It's what he'd done with the party. Going along with Brenda's plans because saying no to her felt harder than keeping a secret from January.

And it's what he'd almost done this morning. Letting January leave without fighting for her because his pride was hurt.

Well, fuck that.

Cam pulled up Brenda's number and pressed call before he could talk himself out of it.

She answered on the second ring. "Cameron, sweetheart. I've been sitting here feeling terrible about that call this morning. January was so upset."

"That's what I need to talk to you about, Miss Brenda," Cam said. "The surprise party is a bad idea and I don't think trying to force or guilt January into coming is productive."

"I know." Brenda sighed deeply. "I heard it in her voice. She really doesn't want this, does she?"

"No, ma'am. She doesn't."

"Oh, Cameron. I just wanted to show her how loved she is. I thought if I could get everyone together, she'd see that her worth isn't tied to some corporate job."

"I know your heart was in the right place. But Miss Brenda, I need to understand something. January's aversion to parties... it feels like more than just not liking attention. Do you know why she feels this way?"

Brenda was quiet for a long moment. "She's always been private. Even as a little girl. Never liked a fuss."

"But this feels deeper than that," Cam pressed gently. "Like it's connected to something specific."

Another pause. Then Brenda's voice changed, as if a memory was surfacing. "Oh my God. Cameron...January's always been that way, ever since she was a little girl, but I never thought about when it started."

"When was that?"

"She was ten. I threw her a birthday party. Invited her whole class, had a cake made, decorations, everything." Brenda's voice grew softer. "It was New Year's Day, and there was an ice storm warning. Not a single child showed up because their parents wouldn't risk the roads."

Cam winced as his heart broke for that little girl. "Poor kid."

"She never complained. Never said she was disappointed. She just smiled and said she understood about the weather, that we could have cake just the three of us." Brenda exhaled. "I thought she was being mature about it. I thought she understood it was the storm, not her. But Cameron...what if a ten-year-old girl saw an empty room and thought no one wanted to come?"

"She's been carrying that ever since."

"And I never knew." Cam could hear Brenda crying now. "I never connected it. She stopped asking for parties after that, but I just thought she'd outgrown them. Oh God, my poor baby. Every birthday since then must have felt like a risk. What if people don't show up again? What if they're just being polite? What if she's not worth the effort?"

"She thinks she's not worth celebrating," Cam said quietly, the pieces falling into place.

"No wonder she ran away," Brenda said. "I was trying to show her how loved she is, and instead I triggered every fear she's been carrying since she was a child. God, no wonder she was so angry. She must hate me now."

Cam thought about the woman he loved. Brilliant, capable January who could manage complex product launches but couldn't accept that she deserved to be celebrated. Who could advocate fiercely for others but struggled to ask for what she wanted for herself.

"She doesn't hate you. She just doesn't want to have this party."

Brenda sighed. "I guess I should go ahead and cancel it...I hate to do this at the last minute but it's the right thing to do."

"Maybe you don't need to cancel, maybe you can make it smaller or..."

Brenda didn't speak for a beat. "Maybe we can. It is technically New Year's. And I know the family with plane tickets won't be able to get refunds," she paused then said, "You know what, Cam, you gave me a brilliant idea...this can be a family reunion."

"And make it clear that January can join by video if she wants to," Cam added. "No pressure to be there in person, no spotlight on her. Just an option to connect with family who love her."

"That's perfect." Brenda's voice strengthened with purpose. "I can call it a New Year's family reunion. January can pop in via Zoom and say hi if she feels like it. No expectations, no forcing her into anything."

"Exactly."

"Cameron?"

"Yes, ma'am?"

"Are you going to tell her what you did?"

Cam looked out at the ocean, where the sun was beginning its descent toward the horizon. "I'm going to try. If she'll listen to me."

"She'll listen. I saw how she looked at you at her father's birthday dinner this summer." Brenda's voice softened. "And I see how you look at her. You're good for each other, sweetheart. You just need to be brave enough to fight for it."

"I'm trying to be."

"I know. And Cameron? Thank you. For caring about her enough to tell me the hard truth."

After they hung up, Cam sat on the beach for a long moment, watching the waves roll in. He thought about that ten-year-old January, smiling bravely while her heart broke. Convinced that she wasn't worth the effort, that people wouldn't show up for her if given the choice.

He pulled up his messages and started typing:

> CAM: Talked to your mom. The surprise party is now a New Year family reunion. No pressure on you, no surprise element. You can join by video if you want, or not at all. Your choice.

He hit send before he could second-guess himself.

Two minutes later, his phone buzzed.

JANUARY: Thank you.

Cam stared at the two words. Not forgiveness, exactly, but acknowledgment. A crack in the wall she'd built between them.

He typed carefully:

CAM: Can we talk?

The response took longer this time. Cam held his breath, watching the three dots appear and disappear, appear and disappear.

JANUARY: Yes. Can you come here? There's a garden behind the house at Sea La Vie. I'll meet you there at 8.

Another message appeared:

JANUARY: The address is 47 Ocean View Drive. Just follow the path around to the back when you get here.

Cam checked his watch. Seven-thirty. Just enough time to shower and change into something that didn't smell like regret and expensive hotel soap.

CAM: I'll be there.

He stood up, brushing sand from his khakis. No grand gestures, no gifts to smooth things over. Just himself and the truth he should have told months ago.

In thirty minutes, he'd either be holding the woman he loved, or watching her walk away forever.

His heart hammered against his ribs as he headed back to the hotel. He'd spent three years being careful, being patient, waiting for the right moment to tell January how he felt.

Maybe it was time to stop waiting and start fighting.

Chapter Thirteen

January

January stood in Sea La Vie's garden, checking her phone for the third time in five minutes. Seven fifty-eight. Cam would be here any minute.

The garden stretched out before her, bougainvillea climbing the trellises and palm trees swaying in the evening breeze. Fairy lights were strung overhead, casting a warm glow as the sun finished setting. She could smell plumeria and hear the ocean in the distance.

She'd changed out of the aqua floral sundress from this morning's disaster into a simple coral short set. She'd braided her hair earlier and now her hair was loose around her shoulders with soft waves from the braids. A touch of lip gloss completed her look. This conversation needed honesty, not armor.

Earlier, Cheryl had squeezed her hand and said, "Trust yourself, love. You know what you need."

Now, standing alone with the fairy lights overhead, January

felt surprisingly calm. The afternoon in the hammock with Cheryl had given her clarity. Cam's text about fixing the party had shown her he could choose her needs over his comfort.

The question was whether it was enough.

Footsteps on the stone path made her turn, and there was Cam, handsome in khaki shorts and a green button-down. His hands were in his pockets and he looked nervous. Their eyes met, and for a moment, neither of them spoke.

"Hi," he said finally.

"Hey," January replied, her heart hammering.

Cam looked around the garden, taking in the fairy lights, the lush tropical plants, the smooth wooden bench positioned between two towering bird of paradise plants. "This is beautiful."

"Cheryl has good taste." January gestured to the bench. "Want to sit?"

They settled on opposite ends, the space between them feeling both too much and not enough. January could smell his cologne mixed with the plumeria-scented air, could see the way his jaw was tight with tension.

The silence stretched between them, heavy with everything unsaid.

"January, I—" Cam started.

"Let me go first," January interrupted, needing to get this out before she lost her nerve. "I need to apologize."

Cam nodded, staying quiet to let her speak.

"I'm sorry for expecting you to read my mind. For never actually setting boundaries with my mother myself. And especially for accusing you of manipulation when I knew—I know—that's not who you are."

She looked down at her hands, at the bracelet he'd given her on Christmas morning still on her wrist. "I was angry and scared and I lashed out at you because you were there. But the truth is, I've spent thirty-nine years expecting other people to fight my battles for me. Expecting them to just know what I need without me having to ask. That's not fair to anyone, least of all you."

Cam was quiet for a moment, and when January looked up, Cam was watching her like he wanted to say everything at once and was afraid to open his mouth. He shook his head, let out a breath, and leaned forward, elbows on knees.

"Thank you for saying that," he said quietly. "But I need to apologize too. I should have spoken up to your mom about the party months ago. When she first told me about it, something in my gut knew you wouldn't want it. But I got caught up in her excitement, and I chose the easy path instead of the right one."

He shifted closer on the bench, his knee almost touching hers. "I told myself I was caught in the middle, that there was no good choice. But that was bullshit. The good choice was being honest with both of you, even if it was uncomfortable. Instead, I kept a secret that hurt you, and I'm so sorry."

January nodded slowly. "I get that it was complicated. But you made a choice, and it hurt me."

"I know that now." Cam reached for her hand tentatively, and when she didn't pull away, he laced his fingers through hers. "I chose comfort over courage. And I almost lost you because of it."

January felt tears prick her eyes. "I was scared too. Scared that what we had was too good to be real. Scared that I'd mess it up somehow. So when I found out about the party, it was easier to be angry than to be vulnerable."

Cam's hand tightened around hers. "Yeah, I get that. I swear, I've spent the last few hours running a greatest hits reel of every way I could've handled all of this better. Honestly? Half of me wanted to just crawl under a rock and text you from there. But then I realized I wanted to see you, take your hand if you'd let me, and I can't do that via text. So here I am."

He looked at her, really looked at her, and January couldn't decide whether to roll her eyes or climb straight into his lap. Maybe both.

"So no more expecting the other person to read our minds. We talk things out, even if it's hard or awkward...agreed?"

"Agreed." Cam's thumb stroked along her knuckles, and January felt warmth spread through her chest.

"Speaking of awkward...Cam, I need to tell you something." January turned to face him fully, drawing strength from his hand in hers. "I've been falling in love with you. Maybe for about a year now, maybe longer. I kept telling myself we were just friends, that it was just attraction, but the truth is... you're the person I want to call when something good happens. You're the person I trust with my fears. You're the person I want beside me when I'm building this next chapter of my life."

Cam grinned at her. "I meant what I said on Christmas Eve. I love you. I've loved you for three years. And I'm not going anywhere."

"Even if 'not going anywhere' means long distance for a while?" January asked. "Because Cheryl offered me a partnership. She wants help launching a line of spa products for Sea La Vie—locally sourced, supporting women in the community. I'd get equity and flexibility to work from anywhere."

"Baby, that sounds amazing," Cam said immediately. "And it sounds exactly like something you'd be brilliant at."

"It would mean splitting my time between here and Atlanta for a while. Maybe a few months to get everything set up and launched."

"Hey, we'll figure it out." Cam's voice was certain. "Video

calls, visits, me taking more vacation than I've ever taken in my life. But we can do this."

January's heart skipped. "You really mean that?"

"Of course. January, I didn't fly to Barbados and bare my soul just to lose you over distance." He cupped her face gently with his free hand. "I choose you. Over comfort, over convenience, over anything else. I choose you."

"I choose you too," January whispered.

Cam leaned forward and kissed her softly, and January melted into him. When they pulled apart, she was smiling through tears.

"There's something else," January said. "The family video call. The New Year's reunion thing you and my mom worked out. Thank you for doing that, by the way," she hesitated, then pushed forward. "I think I want to do it. And I'd like to introduce you to everyone you haven't met. If you're okay with that."

Cam put a hand to his chest. "I'd be honored."

"Speaking of which," Cam said, brushing a strand of hair from her face, "happy early fortieth birthday."

January looked around the garden, taking in the fairy lights twinkling overhead, the man she loved sitting beside her, and the promise of a future she was finally brave enough to claim.

"It already is," she said, and kissed him again.

This time when they pulled apart, Cam stood and pulled her up with him. "What do you want right now?" he asked. "Tell me what you want, and it's yours."

January smiled, remembering Cheryl's words about asking for what she wanted. "I want you to kiss me properly in this garden. I want to fall asleep in your arms tonight. And I want to wake up tomorrow and start building our life together."

"I can do all of that," Cam said, wrapping his arms around her waist.

"But first," January said, standing on her tiptoes, "I want you to kiss me like you mean it."

Cam grinned and obliged, pulling her close as the fairy lights twinkled above them and the ocean waves crashed against the shore. January wrapped her arms around his neck, losing herself in the kiss, in the moment, in the promise of everything to come.

When they finally broke apart, breathless and smiling, January rested her forehead against his.

"Thank you," she whispered.

"For what?"

"For flying across the ocean to find me. For being brave enough to tell me how you felt. For fighting for us when I was too scared to fight for myself."

"Always," Cam said, pressing a kiss to her forehead. "I'll always fight for you. But I love that you're learning to fight for yourself too."

January took his hand and led him toward the path back to the villa. "Come on. Let's go fall asleep in each other's arms."

"Best idea you've had all day," Cam said, following her.

As they walked hand in hand through the garden, past the bougainvillea and plumeria, under the twinkling fairy lights, January felt something she hadn't felt in a long time.

Peace. Joy. Hope.

At almost forty, she was finally becoming the person she was meant to be. Not perfect, not without fears, but brave enough to ask for what she wanted.

And what she wanted was this: a partnership with Cheryl, a relationship with Cam, and the freedom to write her own story on her own terms.

The next chapter was going to be her best one yet.

Epilogue

January 3rd

The week between Christmas and New Year's had passed in a blissful blur. January and Cam had spent their days exploring Barbados—swimming at the stunning pink sands of Crane Beach, watching the dramatic Atlantic waves crash against the rugged rocks at Bathsheba, and venturing underground to marvel at the limestone formations at Harrison's Cave. Nights had been spent dancing at the lively bars along St. Lawrence Gap and, on Friday, devouring grilled fish at Oistins Fish Fry while a local band played soca music under the stars.

They'd stayed at Sea La Vie, falling into an easy rhythm that felt like playing house. January worked with Cheryl on product development plans, sampling prototypes and brainstorming brand positioning. Cam had surprised them both by offering to help Cheryl plan out her e-commerce site, spending hours with his laptop on the villa's veranda, mapping out user flows and payment systems while January brought him coffee and kissed the top of his head.

It felt like building a life together, one beach day and late-night conversation at a time.

Now, waking up on the morning of January 3rd—her actual birthday—January felt something she'd never felt before on this day: genuine excitement.

January woke to sunlight streaming through the windows of her room at Sea La Vie and Cam's arm draped over her waist. She smiled, feeling him stir beside her.

"Morning, birthday girl," Cam murmured, his voice rough with sleep.

"Morning." January turned to face him. "I can't believe I'm actually happy about turning forty."

"That's because forty looks good on you." He pressed a kiss to her forehead. "What do you want to do today? It's your day."

"I've decided I want to join the not-birthday New Year's party remotely, at least for a few minutes. It'll be nice to see everyone."

She gave him a tentative smile. "And I want the rest of my family to meet you...if you're cool with that?"

Cam's smile widened, the corners of his eyes crinkling in that way that made January's heart do a little flip. "Yeah, I can do that. Hopefully your mother's put in a good word or two for me."

"You can do no wrong in her eyes, so you'll be fine. I will warn you though, my Aunt Celeste is going to get all up in your business."

He froze. "Why? What do you mean?"

"Just that she's going to ask you a million questions about your intentions, your job, your credit score...the works." January traced lazy circles on his chest, enjoying the way his muscles tensed slightly under her touch. "She means well, but she has zero filter."

"I mean, who knows what will happen at PeachTech this year, but I guess I'm solid on two out of three."

January raised an eyebrow. "You're solid on your intentions with me?"

Cam's expression shifted, becoming more serious as he propped himself up on his elbow. The playful morning banter had given way to something deeper, and January's pulse quickened as she waited for his response.

"As a rock."

January felt a flutter in her chest at his words. It wasn't just what he said, but the certainty in his eyes that made her believe him completely.

"Whew, Cameron Carter, I do like the sound of that," she whispered, leaning in to kiss him softly.

Later that afternoon, January and Cam sat side by side on the bed, her laptop open in front of them. They'd both dressed up a bit—January in a turquoise sundress that made her skin glow, Cam in a crisp white button-down that made him look unfairly handsome.

"Ready?" she asked.

"Ready."

January clicked the link her mother had sent, and suddenly the screen filled with her family's smiling faces. The venue behind them was decorated with a New Year's theme: black, silver, and gold balloons, streamers, and a banner that read "Happy New Year!" Her mother stood front and center, wearing a glittery gold cowboy hat that was so quintessentially Brenda that January had to laugh.

"January! Happy birthday, baby!" Brenda pressed her hand to her chest. "And there's Cameron...oh, you two are glowing!"

"Hi, Mom. Hi everyone!" January waved at the screen, seeing her father, Aunt Celeste, Uncle Roy, and various cousins crowded around. "Merry... well, Happy New Year, I guess."

"You look wonderful, sweetheart, happy birthday," her father said. "That island life got you right."

"Living your best life, I see," Aunt Celeste chimed in, adjusting her sequined glasses to get a better look at the screen. "And who's that handsome man beside you?"

January felt Cam shift slightly beside her, his knee brushing against hers in a gesture of solidarity. She took a deep breath.

"Everyone, this is Cameron Carter. Cam, this is my family."

January heard her mom tell everyone that she and Cam used to work together and that he was a tech whiz.

"So you're the one who convinced our girl to take a vacation," Uncle Roy said with approval. "Good man. She works too hard."

"Actually, Uncle Roy, taking this trip was all January's idea. I just followed her here because I couldn't stand the thought of her being alone during a difficult time."

Aunt Celeste leaned closer to her camera, studying Cam with the intensity of a seasoned prosecutor. "Cameron, baby, what's your credit score?"

"Aunt Celeste!" January groaned while Cam tried not to laugh.

"What? It's a valid question!"

"Celeste, go open another bottle of champagne and get out the young folks' business." Brenda pushed her way back to the center of the screen, her eyes shining with tears. I'm just so happy for both of you. Cameron, you're family now.

You're coming to Sunday dinner when you get back, you hear me?"

"Yes, ma'am," Cam said. "I wouldn't miss it."

"January, tell us what you've been up to," her father said. "Your mother mentioned something about a business venture?"

January took a deep breath, feeling Cam's supportive presence beside her. "I've partnered with the woman who owns the villa where I'm staying. We're launching a line of spa products locally sourced from Barbados, supporting women in the community. I'll have equity in the business and the flexibility to work from anywhere."

Her father's face lit up with pride. "That's my girl. Building something of your own instead of making somebody else rich. I'm proud of you, sweetheart. If you need investors, you let me know."

"Thanks, Daddy." January felt tears prick her eyes. "That means everything."

"So let me get this straight," Rico said, grinning. "You got fired, flew to Barbados, started a business, and got the man. That's what I call a comeback story."

"When you put it that way..." January laughed, leaning into Cam.

"Actually," Cam said, his voice taking on a more serious tone as he looked at January, "I'm the one who got lucky. Your daughter is the strongest, smartest, most amazing woman I've ever met. I'm crazy about her. Have been for a long time."

The screen went silent for a beat, then Brenda started fanning herself with her hand. "Okay, now you're trying to make me cry on camera, Cameron Carter."

"He's a keeper, January," Aunt Celeste called out. "Even without knowing his credit score."

"I'm keeping him," January said, looking at Cam with a soft smile.

They talked for another thirty minutes catching up with cousins, hearing about Uncle Roy's new car, listening to her mother's plans for renovating the guest bathroom. It felt normal and warm and exactly what January needed.

When they finally said their goodbyes, January closed the laptop and turned to Cam.

"That went well," she said.

"Better than well. Your family is amazing." Cam stood up, stretching. "Now, I need you to get ready for dinner."

"Dinner?"

"It's your birthday. I made plans." He was being purposefully vague, a small smile playing at his lips.

"What kind of plans?"

"The kind where you don't ask questions and just trust me." He kissed her forehead. "Wear something comfortable. We're going to the beach."

An hour later, as the sun began its descent, Cam led January down a path to a private section of beach near Sandy Lane. She'd changed into a simple white sundress, and her hair was loose around her shoulders.

"Cam, what are we—" January stopped abruptly as the beach came into view.

A table had been set up on the sand, covered with white linens and surrounded by tiki torches.

Cheryl and Jianna stood nearby, both grinning as January approached.

"Surprise!" Jianna called out. "Happy birthday!"

"You did this?" January turned to Cam, her eyes wide.

"I had help," Cam said, nodding toward Cheryl. "I wanted you to have a celebration that actually felt like you. Small, intimate, with people who matter."

January felt tears sting her eyes as she took in the scene. The table was set with champagne glasses and a beautiful chocolate cake decorated with tropical flowers sat in the center.

"Jianna made the cake," Cheryl said, putting an arm around the young woman. "And I provided the champagne."

"This is perfect," January whispered, looking at the three people who'd become so important to her in such a short time. "This is exactly what I wanted."

They settled around the table as the sun painted the sky in shades of orange and pink. Cheryl poured champagne, and they cut into Jianna's cake—rich chocolate with a hint of rum and passion fruit.

"Tell us stories," January said, feeling warm and content. "Tell me about the craziest guest you've ever had at Sea La Vie."

Cheryl laughed. "Oh, where do I start?"

They spent the next hour sharing stories and laughter, the conversation flowing as easily as the champagne. Jianna talked about her dreams of running her own property someday. Cheryl shared the story of why she'd left London. Cam told them about his most embarrassing moment at PeachTech, which involved a busted zipper, a presentation to the board, and a strategically placed coffee mug supplied by January.

"Oh, shit, I forgot about that! You were freaking out and I gave you my favorite mug." January laughed.

"That's when I knew," Cam said, looking at January across the table. "That you were the person I wanted in my corner for everything."

As the evening deepened and the stars began to appear, January looked around at the faces illuminated by torch light and felt something settle in her chest. This was what forty was supposed to feel like. Not perfect, not without uncertainty, but full of people who saw her clearly and loved her anyway.

"I want to make a toast," January said, standing up with her champagne glass. The others followed suit.

"To new beginnings," she started, then paused. "No, that's not quite right. To next chapters. To building something that's actually ours. To partnerships—in business and in life." She looked at Cam, her heart full. "To asking for what we want and being brave enough to go after it."

"To January," Cheryl added. "Who reminded me why I started Sea La Vie in the first place. Thank you for bringing your brilliant mind and your generous heart to this business."

"To January," Jianna echoed. "For showing me what it looks like to start over and create something amazing."

"To January," Cam said, his eyes never leaving hers. "For finally seeing what everyone else has always known. You're worth celebrating. Every single day, but especially today."

They clinked glasses, and January felt the tears she'd been holding back finally spill over.

"Happy birthday to me," she whispered, laughing through the tears.

"Happy birthday, baby," Cam said, pulling her close and kissing her softly.

As they sat back down to finish their cake, January looked out at the dark ocean, as she listened to the waves and the easy conversation around her. Contentment washed over her and she sighed softly.

"What are you thinking about?" Cam asked quietly.

January smiled. "That forty isn't an ending. It's just the beginning of the best chapter yet."

"Damn right it is," Cam said, squeezing her hand.

Cheryl raised her glass one more time. "To the best chapter yet."

The Love, Lies, and Catfish Series

Book 1

To Catch a Catfish

London Lewis is back in her childhood home, nursing a broken heart and living with her father and his sinister cat. Newly promoted at Exposé, a firm that specializes in unmasking online dating scams, London is eager to prove herself. Her first client is Donovan Willis, a man convinced that his grandmother's mysterious new suitor is a dangerous catfish.

Despite the seriousness of their investigation, Donovan and London find themselves drawn to each other. Their growing connection becomes harder to ignore, but they both know that mixing personal feelings with professional duties could complicate things.

Can they uncover the truth before it's too late, or will their discovery lead to unexpected consequences?

Book 2

Catfish in Paradise

Aja Lewis has her life figured out. She's built Exposé into Atlanta's premier digital investigation firm, she's got a team she trusts, and she's learned that the only hearts worth protecting are the ones that pay her consulting fees. She also hasn't taken a vacation in four years, but who's counting?

Then her estranged mother dies, leaving behind a mystery that threatens to unravel everything Aja thought she knew about her family.

Del Parris, her mother's laid-back life coach, has answers and an annoying habit of seeing straight through her carefully constructed walls. When their search for truth leads them to Barbados, the uptight workaholic meets her match in a man who thinks "island time" is a perfectly valid schedule and that life's too short for five-year plans.

Between beachside rum tastings and sunset strolls that feel like therapy sessions, Aja discovers that sometimes the best investigations are the ones that lead you back to yourself. And sometimes the most unexpected love stories are the ones that start with letting your guard down.

Also by Joi Jackson

Silver Santa

A single dad with a newly empty nest.

A strait-laced guidance counselor with one birthday wish.

This Christmas, a steamy second chance romance twenty years in the making is about to ignite.

Gia and Winston's friendship is tested when Gia discovers Dre, her one-night stand from Nashville, has moved to Kissing Springs. With both men vying for her heart, will Gia choose her best friend or take a chance with a younger man?

Lovie, a go-getter publicist, eyes a game-changing book tour for a social media sensation. Only snag? Saxon, owner of a bookstore/bourbon bar, won't endorse his ex-wife's juicy tell-all.

Tara, a driven 911 operator, has always kept her feelings for Levi, her older brother's best friend, hidden. But when a string of suspicious fires erupts across town, Tara finds herself working closely with Levi, the town's new arson inspector.

Levi is engaged, but haunted by doubts and growing feelings for Tara, the one woman he's supposed protect, not pursue. As the fires intensify and secrets come to light, Tara and Levi must navigate a web of deceit and danger, risking everything to expose the truth. In the end, they'll have to decide if they're willing to cross the line from friends to lovers.

www.ingramcontent.com/pod-product-compliance
Lightning Source LLC
Chambersburg PA
CBHW031544310726
48971CB00008B/2613